# Abandoned on Everest

## Books by Charles G. Irion and Ronald J. Watkins

The Summit Murder Mystery Series
*Murder on Everest*
*Abandoned on Everest (a prequel to Murder on Everest)*
*Murder on Elbrus (Summer 2010)*
*Murder on Mt. McKinley (Winter 2011)*
*Murder on Puncak Jaya (Summer 2011)*
*Murder on Aconcagua (Winter 2012)*
*Murder on Vinson Massif (Summer 2012)*
*Murder on Kilimanjaro (Winter 2013)*

## Books by Charles G. Irion

*Remodeling Hell*
*Autograph Hell*
*Car Dealer Hell*
*Divorce Hell*
*Roadkill Cooking for Campers (Wild Game Cookbook)*

## Books by Ronald J. Watkins

*Unknown Seas*
*Birthright*
*Cimmerian*
*Evil Intentions*
*Against Her Will*
*A Suspicion of Guilt*
*A Deadly Glitter*
*Alter Ego*
*Shadows and Lies*
*High Crimes and Misdemeanors*

# Abandoned on Everest

## The Shocking True Story of the Doomed Derek Sodoc Expedition

Quentin Stern

as told to
### Charles G. Irion
and
### Ronald J. Watkins

IRION BOOKS

www.AbandonedOnEverest.com
www.IrionBooks.com

iRiON BOOKS

Cover Design by Johnny Miguel, www.johnnymiguel.com
Book Design by The Printed Page, www.theprintedpage.com

Irion Books

480-699-0068
4462 E. Horseshoe Rd.
Phoenix, Arizona 85028
email: charles@charlesirion.com

www.IrionBooks.com

Printed in the United States of America

*Dedicated to those who love scandals,
misdeeds, and revenge!*
—Quentin Stern

# About The Author

We joined Quentin Stern in the release of this book with some trepidation. Our hesitation has to do with what we kindly describe as Stern's "checkered" career and what critics have described as his rather cavalier use of sources. Still, we've decided this work has some merit. Having decided to proceed, some explanation is in order.

Quentin Stern comes from what became the Silicon Valley in Northern California. His parents were well to do; his father owned a large fish distributorship in the Central Valley. Stern spent his formative years laboring in the fish factory, work he abhorred. He attended a well-regarded prep school, but was expelled during his second year for setting the chemistry lab on fire one weekend. After graduating from a public high school, he attended Fresno State College, working on a degree in journalism.

Dropping out of college a semester shy of his degree, he took a job selling advertising and writing articles for a Central Valley shopping mall weekly. His first break came when he relocated to New York and talked his way into a job at the *New York Examiner*, starting as the mail boy. This was a propitious time for the newspaper as it had just been acquired by Michael

Sodoc, who was eager to make it an integral part of his media empire. From all accounts, Stern was aggressive in landing a reporter job, dropping off articles he'd written at night, currying favor with anyone in a position to hire him.

The newspaper and Stern were a perfect fit, it seems. Every skill he's come to rely on since came to him in the dog-eat-dog world of the Manhattan dailies. Stern soon earned a byline and the first stories began to surface about his methods. More than one source claimed to have been misquoted and several denied ever being interviewed. Fellow reporters accused him of stealing stories.

But for all the smoke, nothing came of it. He prospered at the paper and, three years later, took a job as a background reporter for the Sodoc News Service. He's vague about why he made the switch. It may be, as some critics have charged, that he was getting out while the getting was good, or, as he says, he was looking to make a change. Regardless, at SNS he had no on-air time; he worked as a combination researcher/writer of special features.

Away from the newspaper, however, his competitive nature and hard-edged personality did not wear well. Before the year was out, he was let go, only to land a job in Florida with the *National Inquisitor*.

From reporter to television journalist, he found himself a tabloid writer and it was in this role that he hit his stride. Here, it seems, there were fewer questions about sources and methods. He soon began a popular series of stories on Tarja Koivisto, several years before she married Derek Sodoc, about whom he also wrote. So it was natural following the adventurer's tragic death that Stern should be recruited to write this tell-all. From tabloid journalist, he was now a writer of an exposé.

This book draws on personal interviews with some of the participants. Other interviews took place by telephone, e-mail, or ICQ. Any number of articles was written after the event, and the careful reader should notice their inclusion without direct attribution. A number of climbers that year maintained blogs and Stern has acknowledged drawing on them as well.

To the best of our knowledge, this is a reasonably accurate account of the events. Stern was not on the Sodoc expedition, though on occasion he writes as if he was. This is also an intimate account, occasionally told in the first person. Understandably, some sources wished not to be identified. Accusations and innuendo relating to sexual indiscretions and drug use have been on the Internet for months and have appeared in any number of published stories. Stern has shed fresh light on them and the role they may well have played in so many deaths.

In part, Stern says, that's why he wrote *Abandoned on Everest*: to expose those he says are responsible for climbers dying. When pressed, he laughingly admits the advance had a lot to do with it. Finally, he claims he wrote the book because it was "fun."

We consider this to be a valuable contribution to contemporary history and if it is not the final word on those unfortunate events, it is nonetheless a version of them worth telling and considering.

But from what Stern says, it's not over. "This story is unfinished," he told us. "I have the distinct feeling the other shoe has yet to drop. When it does, I'll be there. That's one story I want to tell firsthand."

Charles G. Irion
Ronald J. Watkins

# Introduction

International adventurer Derek Sodoc was shamefully abandoned and left to die on the deadly, snowy summit of Everest.

That's the simple truth of this life and death. Until now, no one has had the courage to tell the sordid facts. Instead, judicious lies, endless excessive media hype, and obviously self-serving statements have passed themselves off for reality. "They're all afraid to tell what really happened," a source close to the story revealed to me. "The reality is so much worse than the lies."

As is always the case in life, the truth is much stranger than mere fiction—in this case, far, far stranger. Stories from the slopes of the mountain describe drug addiction, sexual misadventures, pregnancy, abortion, cowardice, theft of vital equipment, and sabotage. It is a sordid, seedy tale. No wonder so many people have worked so hard to keep you, the public, from learning it. "They're afraid of the father," the same source confided. "I know that I am."

Imagine, if you will, the tragic fate of one of the world's richest and most famous glittering—if ill-starred—celebrities. This is a man who should have lived a long sunlit life and died comfortably between silken sheets at his estate, surrounded by his youthful fourth wife, numerous children, and handwringing accountants. That's the way of it with the unbelievably rich. But it was not fated to be.

"Derek loved life," the source said. "But he was determined to climb Everest. In those final days, however, he was obsessed with his wife and the new man in her life."

As a result, Derek Sodoc died a miserable, inglorious death, just yards from his lifelong goal, the precipitous peak of the world's highest—and often deadliest—mountain. How is such a thing even possible? I ask that question because Derek Sodoc had it all, certainly by the standards of the rest of us. He could afford the finest in technology, the latest in scientific equipment, the most skilled and accomplished stalwart guides. He took with him as well his most steadfast friends, rugged men who'd demonstrated their mettle before, stout men he knew he could rely on in a pinch.

His death should never have happened—not then, not there.

Yet in the final agonizing hours of his all-too-short life, those well-paid minions and erstwhile friends turned their yellow tails and fled down the craggy mountain rather than rescue their gilded client and alleged friend. "Like rats abandoning a sinking ship," an insider told me, "the bunch of them hot-footed it down that mountain. They didn't let anyone stand in their way or care who they left behind."

Wrapped in the inescapable cold and trapped in one of the worst blizzards in recorded history, Derek valiantly clung to life until finally succumbing to the overwhelming odds against him. Where were his friends? Where were the expensive guides?

He died alone and abandoned.

~~~

This is the true story of what happened on that ill-starred, disastrous expedition, and in particular on that final tragic day.

Drawn from sources who witnessed events, this is unadulterated reality, unvarnished by media hype. "The truth," one source says, "would turn your stomach."

Yet it is said that the truth will set you free. This truth, unpopular as it is, should set free any number of liars. Watch them squirm.

For example, where was Derek's wife as he lay dying? One of the world's most gifted female athletes, Tarja Sodoc was to have climbed Everest with him. Many women were more than willing to have joined him on this glorious adventure and would have risked their lives to save him, but she did not.

So where was she that last, deadly day? Why wasn't she on the final summit team as intended? What was she doing? What else was so important to her? For weeks, the expedition trumpeted that the husband and wife would reach that forbidding, towering summit together, but on the final tragic day, she was nowhere to be seen.

What happened? And why won't she talk? Is it true that she was keeping warm in her own little high-altitude love nest? That is what those who were there say.

And what about Dr. Calvin Seavers, Derek's longtime friend and expedition physician? Where was he? Why is he silent? Or Scott Devlon, war hero and presumed fast friend? Why has he refused comment? What is he hiding?

"If talking would save their necks, they'd speak up," an informed source says. "You can bank on it."

And what about all the others—why stand on their silence? What is it they seek to conceal? What dark secrets do they hide? Why are they afraid?

---

This is the shocking story of how one of the world's richest men was callously abandoned to his miserable fate on one of the deadliest points on earth. This is a story of self-serving betrayal, a shameful tale of loss—and it is a shocking story of unbridled lust.

You may think that you know what happened, but you don't. Now, for the first time, the truth can be told. It's not a pretty story, and it's certainly not a happy one. It's a lurid tale and one that everyone is entitled to know.

# Chapter One

# The Silver Spoon

The super-rich, it is said, are born with a silver spoon in their mouths. I don't know the saying's origin, but it's better than a kick in the mouth and the point is still valid: the lucky children of the rich have it better than the rest of us. It's not fair, but that's the way of the world.

But being a commoner is not without its perks. What our lowly status grants us is a seat on the comfortable bleacher of life, where from our perch we can observe the foibles and stupidities of those born with every advantage. There are reasons why the rest of us can't always get ahead in life. Born to impoverished parents, we may be denied a proper education. Lacking money, we will have been denied the greater cultural experiences that enrich life and broaden our useful circle. All of this serves to limit our present and our future. They, on the other hand, have no excuses for failure. So I wonder sometimes who has the better deal, I really do.

"You can't imagine the kind of life the very rich live, you really can't," one Derek pal recently told me. "If people saw it, they'd hang the bunch."

We watch celebrities spring from nothing like mildew in your basement, like the Hollywood walk-on waiting on tables who is suddenly a superstar. We learn all about them: who they date, what they do, what they like and don't like, who they think we should vote for. We dress like them, we pay to see and hear them, we dream about *being* them or having sex with them. It's voyeurism at its best—or worst.

Then we sit back and watch them fall. Drugs, alcohol, sex, gambling, egotism, all of the sins and then some, and wonder what it would be like, both the climb and the fall. The seamy tabloids tear them apart and, for most of us, the wanton destruction of someone famous is a lot more fun than the meteoric rise. They get what they deserve, all of them; that's what we say and take satisfaction in believing.

Though not a perfect human being, Derek Sodoc was someone we'd genuinely like to have known. Given his background and upbringing, that is extraordinary. From birth, it should have been very different for him. As the only son of perhaps the world's richest man and arguably the most powerful private citizen, Derek led a pampered, privileged life—the kind about which we can only dream. He grew up in mansions, was waited on hand and foot, and attended the most exclusive boarding schools, where he befriended and hobnobbed with the offspring of other rich and powerful men, making the connections that would assure him a lifetime of success.

He also enjoyed exotic vacations to places you and I can only dream about. For his tenth birthday, his father rented Disneyland for a weekend. That's right, the entire theme park. Derek's friends and their families were flown in from around the world for the occasion and housed in the Disneyland Hotel, which the senior Sodoc had also rented exclusively.

The story is that for his sixteenth birthday, his father rented a very different facility—a private mansion in an exclusive Paris neighborhood, reserved for a very special clientele.

Though not a virgin, he spoke to friends about that night for the rest of his life.

"He used to joke about it," a close pal said. "How he'd just as soon hang out with the guys on a public beach, but people expected this way of life from him. How it wasn't possible for him to just be normal. Not that he minded the perks, not one bit."

As if any other examples were needed, his father owned a Greek island named Aphrodite Ourania. That's right, his very own Greek island. There the senior Sodoc had specially built a rustic Greek fishing village, with every convenience of the twenty-first century hidden behind the stone walls. Just as Marie Antoinette played at being an Austrian milkmaid in a humble *faux* village behind her lavish mansion, so too did Michael Sodoc enjoy retreats to his Greek island. He was joined there by Italian starlets, supermodels, Asian movie stars; you name her, if she was young, beautiful, and famous, she spent some time with him on that island paradise. If one in ten stories about what goes on there is true, it deserves a hundred books; but you don't write about Michael Sodoc—not in an honest way and keep your career. So let's just say the son, Derek, enjoyed his own frolics there, first innocent ones as a child and later those of an adult.

"I was there the night his private jet flew in a trio of Thai movie stars," a source said. "Derek was generous in sharing them."

One Malaysian movie star is a case in point. Derek met her at the World Trade Center in Tokyo, where he'd been sent to represent SNS at a time when he was considering joining his father's media empire. Of Chinese descent, Yue Su was the most popular Asian star outside of Hong Kong. As a child star, she was the darling of Malaysia, making the transition into adult stardom seamlessly. It was vital that she maintain a conservative aura about her and her virginity was assumed well into her twenties.

In fact, she'd had a string of lovers starting when she was still a teenager, all of them directors of her many films or financial backers. Her career was starting to fade when she accepted a fee to represent a Malaysian shipping company at the Tokyo World Trade Center.

"The connection between the two was immediate," a close friend told me. "I've never seen anything like it. They didn't come up for air for three days. And by then, she no longer cared about her public image. The paparazzi were all over them—including the famous shot of her darting out of Derek's suite in her undergarments, her evening dress clutched against her breasts."

Yue's career ended that night; their affair was over two months later. The following year, a tape of Yue engaging in sex with her tycoon boyfriend surfaced on the Internet and the former child star jumped from a Singapore high-rise.

Derek owned in his own right, or had access to, the world's most expensive toys. He sailed what has been described as the world's costliest racing yacht, *Windsong*; flew everywhere in his very own private Gulfstream G550, dubbed "Derek One," and hosted an international adventure television show. All these and much, much more were his by right of birth. The world, in effect, was his private candy store.

As he matured, though, his interest in toys faded. He sold the yacht, his plane sat unused for months, and it is rumored he had to be pushed to record segments for his show. As for the women—well, they were playthings for whom he always found time. And were there ever women: women by the score, drawn to his good looks, to his wealth and to his fame. He dated movie stars, fashion models, daughters of the other rich, even a princess who was widely reported to be interested in marrying him. It was a fairy-tale life and an international playground for any red-blooded man with his fair share of testosterone.

It seemed to us watching from the outside that Derek would never marry, certainly not in the physical prime of his life. Why should he? Marriage offered nothing he didn't have so available that the rest of us could but wonder at it. Derek was, after all, the world's most eligible bachelor, eagerly sought by every international beauty.

Then came his unexpected, and unexplained, marriage to Tarja Koivisto just four months before his death. Where a princess had not been good enough, Tarja, the scheming bed-hopper, was.

"She told him she was pregnant," a close pal says. "She used the oldest trick in the book, then after the wedding she claimed she'd had a miscarriage. I don't think he believed her and that was the beginning of the end."

Others, however, just as well-placed, have their own version of events. "They'd had a three-way. I'm sure it wasn't the first time for him—or her for that matter. In this case, though, it was a problem. The third player was a very young teenage boy. Loaded on drugs, drunk, let's just say Derek did some things he later regretted and Tanya filmed them. It was blackmail, pure and simple." So claims a former employee of the socialite.

"It was herpes," a usually reliable source later wrote. "He gave it to her and she threatened to go public. He married the bitch to shut her up." This seems thin on its face, but who's to say? The only person who knows why Derek married Tarja, really and truly, was Derek, and he's not saying.

It should be easy to be the son of a rich and powerful man and it should have been easy for Derek. All that is required is to sit back and let the world flow to you. There are those who say, and I agree, that the hard part is going your own way when the yellow brick road paved with gold is there before you at conception. All Derek ever had to do in life was show up; everything else was a given.

We don't know what happened between the senior Sodoc and his only son. We don't know why his first wife, Derek's mother, killed herself. Sodoc has never offered a satisfactory explanation for the events of that appallingly tragic night and the official reports have been conspicuously missing from day one. We do know that she was hastily cremated without an autopsy and that the district attorney responsible for any criminal inquiry resigned the following month to accept a very lucrative legal position within the Sodoc media empire. All terribly suspicious, but also the way of the world for the rich and famous. Just recall poor Mary Jo Kopechne.

The consequence of all this Machiavellian orchestration was that Derek grew up without a mother, largely ignored by a man preoccupied with building a personal empire. Surrounded by servants, Derek was reared in the lap of luxury. Poor little rich boy.

It's easy not to feel sympathy for Derek. After all, he had everything. All you have to do is look at the privileges with which he was gifted. But the sad truth is that he was a very lonely boy, raised more by those agreeable servants than his father, looking to teachers to serve as surrogate parents. Examining his life today, it is remarkable that he turned into the fundamentally decent man he became. Not perfect, of course, but decent and good, courageous, the lover women desired, the older brother and friend men instinctively craved.

For all these advantages and a life's path dictated by a controlling, powerful father, Derek found the strength to choose his own way. He turned his back on endless luxury and became an international adventurer.

We know that his father objected. Oh, how he objected! Here was a man whose entire career was built around getting his way.

"They nearly came to blows," a source close to the family confided. "I've never seen Mr. Sodoc so angry. I thought he'd have a stroke right then and there. You have to hand it to Derek. He stood his ground. Not many can against such a man."

The key meeting between the determined father and rebellious son took place in the executive restaurant in Sodoc's worldwide media headquarters. The Sodoc management team spent months preparing for the meeting. The senior Sodoc personally saw to every detail, including the elaborate spread. At the luncheon, he presented a package showing Derek's projected career path at SNS, the salary, the perks, the opportunities. "He was going to learn the business as his father's right-hand man," the source reports. "That had been Sodoc's plan from the day his son was born."

Derek would spend a year simply following his father initially—"carrying the old man's briefcase" was how Derek put it to a friend later. Sodoc's idea was to expose his son to the issues and challenges his father dealt with every day. After that, Derek was to spend a year in Europe, managing the company's expansion from the Paris office. It was a position requiring tact and skill, one Derek would very likely have performed well. "In that regard, Sodoc had the measure of his son," a former senior SNS staffer revealed. "Had Derek followed this path, I have no doubt he'd have excelled in Europe. In many ways, he was always more European than American in his outlook and manner."

A successful year in Europe was to be followed by a year in Singapore. Here Derek was to be given a free hand managing Asian operations—to be cut from the apron strings, so to speak. Having gained confidence in his own right, he was to return to New York to assume control of the global enterprise as president. Sodoc was intending to remain CEO and chairman, but wanted to take a back seat from daily management so he could focus on forward thinking. He was also dating his future wife, the Russian model, and she was taking more and more of his time.

But it was not to be. Derek flatly refused the career path so carefully planned for him. Sources say he was never even tempted. The one person Sodoc had not properly considered in making this decision was his son, the target of all this attention. The young man simply had no interest in following in his father's footsteps. "He wanted his own life," a college friend told me. "He wanted to be successful in his own right, apart from and away from his father."

It came as a bitter blow to the father, a man accustomed to getting his way. He sweetened the deal, made concessions, but it did no good. Derek was determined to have his way. Perhaps, given enough years, Michael Sodoc would have won out, but the one thing his power and wealth couldn't buy was time. Each of us is given his or her measure by Divine Providence; it is not weighed upon earthly scales.

You might say "good for Derek" and you'd be right. Good for Derek. In the end, despite the cornucopia of opportunities provided him by celebrity and riches, he turned to the one great life challenge where money can't buy success or guarantee safety: mountaineering.

The concession Derek made was to accept the assistance of his father's vast media empire in showcasing his exploits. Perhaps he gave that small bone to his father, maybe he was attracted to exposure it would give, or perhaps he was seriously considering a life on camera. We'll never know. But all of his feats were featured on SNS television and the world-wide Sodoc media empire publications. In time, Derek received his own television show, one that showcased his exploits and made him a respected spokesman for environmental causes.

As a mountaineer, Derek followed in the footsteps of adventurer Richard Bass and set about climbing the highest peak on each of the world's seven continents. It became

Derek's goal to climb these mountains, recording his exploits and telecasting from every summit. He had successfully climbed six of them before tackling the toughest nut of all in Everest.

Thorough in preparing for every step he took—except in marriage—he had traveled to Nepal the previous August accompanied by his longtime friend, Doc Calvin. There he met with the finest Everest guide to the world, Reggie Maul, and arranged to hire the best Sherpa guides. He planned his summit of Mt. Everest in every detail over that summer. "There were no parties, scarcely any women," a pal confided. "This was all business. He knew how daunting Everest was and he planned to make his expedition a success. I'm certain that no one was more surprised by the outcome than he was."

"Surprised" is scarcely the word for it.

When it came time to organize the expedition, Derek spared no expense in terms of equipment. Anything that was needed was acquired. The latest climbing gear was assembled, including state-of-the-art line, tents, high-altitude suits, titanium ice axes and ascenders, and medicines. The expedition that set out for the slopes of Everest possessed the latest technology, including satellite telephones that allowed worldwide communication from anywhere on the mountain. Every climber carried a radio that allowed him to be in continuous contact with the expedition leader, Reggie, as well as with one another.

A lanky, amiable New Zealander, Reggie Maul was spending his fifth season as a respected Everest guide, despite a lifelong struggle with alcohol. Lessons from previous Everest disasters were taken to heart, especially those learned in 1996 when so many highly respected climbers perished. It was believed that with new weather predicting programs and digital communications, Everest could now be safely conquered; such is man's hubris. Reggie considered it his life's mission to get every intrepid climber to the top, then get them down alive and in one piece. Until the day of his own death, Reggie had never lost a climber on Everest.

That is the way of it. In good conditions, men climb with no great difficulty and come to believe they have mastered the mammoth mountain. But it is only a pathetic illusion, for we are always within her grasp, allowed to live only at her indomitable will.

Coverage of Derek's other mountain conquests had been aired to high ratings. Anticipation this time was heightened by the fact that he had recently wed Tarja. Their unexpected courtship while climbing Vinson Massif, the highest point in Antarctica, followed by their conquest of Mount Kilimanjaro and their immediate marriage had caught everyone by surprise and mesmerized the portion of the world that knows no better.

We can assume the New York suits dreamed up the ill-conceived plan for the newlyweds to summit together. All very romantic. The athletic couple had met on the slopes of Vinson Massif, not long after Derek had conquered Mount Aconcagua in South America; courted in the wilds of the Serengeti Plain; and been married at sea off Mauritius.

Since the hasty marriage was a reality, SNS sought to exploit the media's obsession with the attractive couple. Every effort was made to broadcast their "heartwarming" story. The ideal was to have been a truly glorious shot of the intrepid pair stepping triumphantly on top of the world at the same moment, all smiles, glowing with the warmth of their combined success, a metaphor for this magnificent union of man and woman.

That was the plan. The reality turned out to be something very different—and very deadly. How much the single-minded push to accomplish that plan led to such appalling deaths— I'll leave for you to judge.

---

Over the last century, many respected climbers have written that it's ill advised to try to accomplish two goals at once on top of Everest. The greatest mountaineers have said, for example, that scientific expeditions should not be mingled with summit attempts. Climbing Mt. Everest is so deadly that you dare not divert your attention to secondary goals. No one at SNS read these books—assuming they can read—or if they did, no one believed them. They were smarter men, they thought, with better technology and more experience. Old rules didn't apply to the chosen elect.

In this first decade of the twenty-first century, Westerners believed that they had conquered nature. There was nothing we could not do if we just set our mind to it and threw enough money at the problem.

And Derek, as well, had come to believe he could do anything.

---

Despite the setback in recruiting his son, Michael Sodoc threw his publicity empire into promoting the expedition. As a consequence, it became a SNS worldwide media event. A camera crew was sent to record every moment, no matter how mundane. That one of the two crew members was a former lover of Derek's who might still be disgruntled was of no concern. Everyone had a job to do and personal considerations meant nothing.

Articles and news accounts have already reported how every aspect of the elaborate expedition was stage-managed like summer stock. Movement from place to place was timed for filming and weather conditions. Editing equipment was included on the expedition so the best possible face could be put on every bit of video. So extensive was the coverage and determined the publicity that even before Derek set foot in magical Nepal, anyone who watched nightly television, browsed the Internet, or read an SNS-owned publication knew that Derek Sodoc was about to conquer the highest point on earth.

It was no secret that the senior Sodoc disapproved of the hasty marriage. His tabloids had covered Tarja's affair with the very rich, maritally challenged Lewis Scarbrough in exacting detail, often including provocative photographs of the lithe young woman in alleged side affairs with sports figures—both male and female. Perhaps he hoped to show his son the photographs he couldn't publish. But Derek had acted so quickly that there was nothing his father could do but grin and bear what was already done.

"No one in the world knew Tarja more intimately than Sodoc did. His reporters and cameras had pried into every crawlspace of her self-centered life. He knew what a detestable human being she truly was," says a source once close to the diva.

But another published report says, "He was jealous, pure and simple. Sodoc had dated her briefly himself and was angry when she dropped him because it was clear he wouldn't marry her. He treated her like a whore and she didn't like it. Whores never do."

"I heard he couldn't keep up with her in the bedroom," still another source wrote on a blog. "He was popping that little blue pill for her, but even that wasn't enough. He liked his women two at a time, but just didn't have the stamina for it any longer. He was stunned and furious when she dropped him."

Given the history, there are pals of Derek who say he may have married this particular woman to spite his father. There are those who claim this was the most conspicuous act of independence in his brief life.

Perhaps it's true. Again, we'll never know.

What we do know is that just four months after their wedding, following their fairy-tale Bora Bora honeymoon, Derek and his new bride arrived in Nepal with several ex-lovers and soon-to-be lovers in tow, all smiles and aglow with love and lust. It was as volatile a mix as ever graced the slopes of any great mountain—and surely the deadliest.

# The Magical Appeal
# of Mt. Everest

*By Marta Espinoza*
*Sodoc News Service*
*May 10*

Climbers returning from the Himalayas all report a similar, near-spiritual experience. "It was like entering a cathedral," one woman wrote. "You feel closer to God."

Since ancient times, mountaintops have been associated with the divine. Holy men are always found atop mountains. It appears to be no different today. "I can't say I'm a wiser or better man for all the mountains I've climbed," Derek Sodoc recently said. "But I believe I am."

The Sodoc Foundation Everest expedition has set out from Kathmandu and is expected to summit Mt. Everest in early June. Once he stands astride the highest point on earth, Derek will have climbed the highest point on each of the world's seven continents.

Though technology provides a greater measure of safety to those seeking to summit Mt. Everest than ever before, climbers still trek up the mountain one painful step at a time. Still, few who attempt the climb have a complaint. "It is magic up there," Derek Sodoc said in a recent speech to the leadership of Greenpeace at the Carlyle Hotel in Manhattan, "and it draws us like a spiritual flame."

Sodoc will plant the Greenpeace flag on the summit.

# Chapter Two

# Trekking to Everest

The Sherpa say that Everest is the goddess of heaven, sometimes called the mother goddess; in their language, she is known as Sagarmatha. For centuries before the Europeans came, the childlike Sherpa gazed in wonder and awe at the imposing goddess mountain. They made devoted offerings, burned musky incense, erected brightly colored prayer flags, knelt in prayer, and trembled in terror at the very thought of breaching her divine flanks.

In the three decades since the conquest of Everest, only a handful of highly skilled climbers attempted to summit, some succeeding, most not. But with improved technology and greater access to the approaches, it became increasingly a feat for celebrities. In 1985, businessman Richard Bass climbed Everest——the first person to climb each of what became known as the Seven Summits. Five years later, the first married couple, from Slovenia, summited together. By the time of the Sodoc expedition, hundreds of Westerners and a like number of Sherpa had climbed the mountain.

So the question is: Why all the hype? Derek was not the first to climb Everest. He was not the first to climb the seven highest mountains on each of the world's continents. And he and Tarja would not have been the first couple to summit together. What was the big deal?

The answer is contained in a name: Michael Sodoc.

Unable to lure his headstrong son into the family business, Sodoc decided to publicize his every endeavor. Doubtless this was an insidious plan to seduce the boy, but we'll never know, though it certainly proves what can be accomplished with enough resources. It demonstrates as well just how much news is generated by the media, produced rather than reported.

---

Everest cannot be conquered in the winter. It is too cold and the storms are too violent. It is impossible even to reach the approach routes of the mountain. Summer is just as bad; the monsoon sweeps in heavy with moisture, producing thick snow as well as violent storms. There is no passage to the peak.

For these reasons, it is possible to climb the mountain only two times of the year. These brief windows of opportunity exist when the weather patterns switch from winter to summer, then from summer to winter. One occurs about May most years—the other, briefer one in the fall. But even those periods are inherently unstable and dangerously unpredictable.

For a short period—sometimes measured in as little as days, rarely more than a few weeks—it can be just possible to climb Mt. Everest, though in some especially violent years even these windows do not appear. This is not to say that when these periods do emerge, the weather is either predictable or benign. Sudden violent storms are routine. Deadly fronts sweep in, outstripping prediction. Equally deadly storms form from the mountain's microclimate, springing up from below without warning. During these windows, few storms last long—yet for the period of their existence, they are extraordinarily violent and deadly.

Derek elected to attempt the summit of Mt. Everest during the month of May. For that reason, his enormous expedition set out from Kathmandu in early April. Tarja arrived first, accompanied by a well-known Parisian model with whom she'd been sporadically involved for the last year. The two were seen everywhere together. There is little nightlife for Westerners in Nepal, but the pair was seen at those that did exist.

"Their behavior was shocking," a local reporter confided in me. "We do not accept such behavior in the kingdom. I have traveled and I know it is common in the West for women to dance together, pretending to be lovers. Even that would have been too much for us. But these two … they did more than dance, you understand. Did I tell you the other woman was African with very dark skin? It was scandalous."

The pair made no secret of the true nature of their relationship. Maids told local reporters what the pair was up to in private, but the newspapers refused to run such articles. Two days before Derek arrived, the model was put on a plane and returned to France. If Derek voiced any objection to his bride's shenanigans, or even knew of them, it has never been publicly disclosed. Tarja soon had him busy enough.

"Tarja discovered a new kind of hashish in Kathmandu and introduced Derek to the stuff," a member of the expedition later wrote. "Given his history of drug use, this was a catastrophe. His friends had been careful to respect his wishes since his last time in a rehab center. We all knew he could be tempted."

For some three years, shortly after college, Derek had used cocaine heavily, according to those who knew him best. Sick of himself and the life he was leading, he spent a summer detoxing in a remote Alpine cabin outside Zürich. It was there that his interest in mountaineering was rekindled. But there had been the inevitable relapses—the last just before he'd gone to

South America. Now, in Nepal, his new wife was encouraging his return to drug use. It was a problem that would nag the expedition.

───※※※───

It's been said that the first landing of a man on the moon received less coverage than did the Sodoc Foundation Everest expedition. No longer must the world await dispatches from remote regions to receive news. With modern communication, it is possible to have images, video, sound, and the latest stories almost as they happen. Now the public sees reality, no longer spoon-fed to them by publicists, and reality is truth, truth the rich and famous often don't want you to know. But when the world's most dominant news source picks its storyline, controls access, and edits every release, truth is often the first casualty.

The international media boisterously clustered at the starting point of the expedition once the buses and trucks were left behind. Every minute of video recorded of Derek was eagerly sought. News outlets from more than a dozen nations dispatched crews to snag those interviews—often including an attractive reporter to persuade him—to make those minutes of interview available by fair means or foul. Once the expedition set out on foot it was joined by other expeditions, each clamoring for video shots and interview time.

The approach trek that year proceeded more like a Mardi Gras procession than anything associated with serious mountaineering. Porters carried loads on their backs interspersed with the slow moving yak, which carried their own burdens. The expedition stretched like a great snake along the trail, winding through diminutive valleys, across tranquil streams, through cultivated fields and orchards, and over the rounded passes of the lower elevations. All along the route, Sherpa turned out in droves to witness the spectacle.

All on the Sodoc Foundation Everest expedition admit it was an exciting time. This event had been anticipated for months. But it was more than merely a story. There is always an air of excitement as you prepare to enter the great unknown, to lay your life on the line, for no other reason than you want to. The same air permeated the entire expedition—from humble porter to skilled climber. Everyone knew this climb was different.

And it didn't take a rocket scientist to figure that out. No athletic achievement in history has been covered in more detail. There were moments when the cameras and microphones outnumbered those being interviewed. Even the most mundane moments were captured on camera. "It was like living in a zoo," a climber said. "People gawking, filming, and recording at all hours. It was very distracting. That's probably why so many died."

The expedition was enormous. Nothing like it had been seen on Everest since the days of the first mammoth British surveying expeditions, when hundreds of climbers and porters had taken to the mountains. Some sixty yak—the animals used by Sherpa to portage supplies to Base Camp—were interspersed with the climbers, bells tinkling, grunting from time to time in their distinct way. Each was led by a herder.

The group also included at least one Sherpa guide for every Western climber. For safety reasons, no climber would be unaccompanied above Base Camp. All these, plus the porters and kitchen help and the five Sherpa assigned to the SNS staff, brought the number of Sherpa alone to more than ninety. Ten Westerners formed the core of the Sodoc Foundation Everest expedition, but this did not include the same number and half again who were part of the other expeditions marching in tandem with the Sodoc expedition.

Consider another expedition of considerable size was marching just ahead—and that the Sodoc expedition was followed by both Italian and Japanese camera crews—and you have some idea of the scope of this endeavor. Every camera shot seemed unique, but cameramen were jockeying for a position that excluded a view of the others. It was not easy.

The expedition in front was from Nepal. Led by Girija Dahal, it was an effort of the national university. Its stated purpose was the study of the impact of so many climbers on that mountain region. Nearly fifty in all were on the expedition. Interestingly, and significantly, Dahal had been one of the escorts for one of the nation's living goddesses, known as the Kumari, the previous summer.

Without the yak, those beasts of burden, there would be no conquest of Everest. The British at first used small Mongolian ponies, but over the years, the yak had emerged as the second preferred conveyor of every necessity, and every luxury, needed for an expedition. The first choice is, of course, the backs of the Sherpa themselves. The poorer and more desperate they are, the more they are compelled to carry until finally they are broken and discarded. But unlike the yaks, they are not eaten, merely abandoned.

Every essential—from tents to bedding, food, and portable potties—was in tow along with every imaginable bit of media technology. The quantities were amazing. These included satellite phones, computers, solar panels to recharge batteries, the latest in portable radios, and lightweight digital cameras, to name a few.

And there were also an enormous quantity of luxuries. These included gourmet foods, alcoholic drinks of every kind, comfortable camp chairs and recliners, additional changes of clothing not required by necessity, beds, video screens not needed for SNS, but for evening DVDs, and an endless list of personal and unnecessary vanity effects.

All of these were portaged through the foothills then up that mountain on the backs of the yak and Sherpa porters. Tarja, for one, had five yak assigned to her alone and sported a different designer outfit every day for the first three weeks of the trek. She also brought her own manicurist/hairstylist, though this woman became ill with mountain sickness and turned back after just one night at Base Camp.

Since the progress to the Base Camp was so slow, both to allow for acclimatization and because of the enormous quantities of everything being hauled, Derek recorded near-daily bits to be beamed to New York. At every picturesque vista, he could be seen being carefully lit before Rusty Landon, Derek's cameraman, began to film. Some of these clips were for use later on his own show, *High Adventure!* and others were meant to air on the evening news or the frequent SNS specials covering the expedition.

Although SNS dominated coverage, allowance was made for the other crews joining the expedition, though these were carefully orchestrated and use privileges meticulously negotiated by the SNS producer, Crystal Hernandez. Those were the rules of the game. Tarja basked in the ceaseless attention, clinging to Derek's side whenever the cameras were directed at him. She possessed, it is reported, a sixth sense for spotting a camera lens no matter how distant.

Initially, it wasn't necessary for her to take advantage of her famous husband since there was as much attention directed at Tarja, the new bride, as toward Derek, the great adventurer. And why not? She was beautiful, athletic, and famous in her own way. While her beauty and athleticism can be attributed to genetics, her fame was entirely her own creation.

It's not possible to have read a magazine or newspaper, or watched a television celebrity show, and not know Tarja Sodoc. The only daughter of college intellectuals, she'd excelled at winter sports. It was thought that she'd represent the United States in the Olympics, but the flirtatious, stunningly beautiful athlete had very different ambitions. With an inheritance from her grandmother, she moved to Manhattan and was soon working the cocktail circuit, meeting the rich and famous.

The story is well known in all its lurid details. In Manhattan, she made the rounds of countless cocktail parties, gaining access with her looks and new friends—to one of whom it is said she paid $100,000 for access. What followed was a campaign of relentless intensity. She came to the attention of the city's most important, influential, and wealthy men. Age didn't matter, nor did appearance. Money was its own aphrodisiac. And marital status? Perish the thought. The richer, the better in her mind and, since divorce has a way of reducing wealth, few of these men were unmarried.

So it was she came in contact with seventy-two-year-old Lewis Scarbrough—perhaps New York's best known real estate developer and philanthropist. It is said that he served as the model for the younger Donald Trump—in more ways than one, it would seem. Scarbrough was an easy enough catch for Tarja; within hours of meeting, they were performing the horizontal mambo.

Tarja hired a publicist and, before Scarbrough could work up a good story about their relationship, it was on the front page of the New York tabloids. For the two torrid years of the steamy relationship, Tarja was the stuff of tabloids. Publicly branded "the other woman," she was famous for nothing so much as her bed hopping. When Scarbrough was out of town the young nymph was seen dancing the night away in nightclubs.

"You have to see her nude to believe it," one former, lucky lover told me. "She has the figure of a goddess, skin like fine porcelain. Those breasts are all real, the nipples firm and rigid when you run your hand over them. Once she gets going, she pants like a steam engine; body heat rolls through her in waves. She's like another creature altogether. But don't look her in those cat's eyes she's got. They're cold, man, *cold*."

Tarja was often seen on the arms of other rich men, though none seemed to take. Perhaps there was something about her that they could detect—a predatory nature behind that dazzling smile and jutting breasts. Still, with her fame, such as it was, she landed several product endorsements and even sold a memoir, *Getting It*, though it found more use as a doorstop than it did on the bookshelf. As trashy books go, it's a window into her soulless mind, scandalously portrayed by her anonymous ghostwriter.

Tarja thrived in the fever swamp of Manhattan, from all appearances never objecting to being branded the other woman. Carrying on an affair with a man three times her age, she was seen gracing the covers of magazines and newspapers nearly every day of the week. She successfully turned adultery into her own personal cottage industry.

When it ended, Tarja coerced a settlement from Scarbrough, then fled New York and has not since returned. Good riddance there. She was connected for a time to various European play-boys: Italians Giorgio Balla and Umberto Chirico, Brazilian Jose da Silva and Spaniard Pedro Luis Rey, allegedly nurs-ing Rey through a heroin overdose. But when the paparazzi stopped following her and the magazines no longer ran her photos, she left Europe, embarking on her ballyhooed cam-paign to climb the Seven Summits. Her mix of beauty and athleticism proved simply irresistible to a certain kind of media, encouraged by her publicist. It was during one such expedition to Antarctica where she stalked, and landed, Derek Sodoc. It was a media frenzy from that point on.

Until the moment of his son's death, the senior Sodoc was working to have the marriage annulled. Derek was expected to follow in the steps of his domineering father, not squander his life with a round-heeled blonde bimbo. That's clearly what Michael Sodoc wanted and there are stories galore to tell you that whatever the senior Sodoc wants, he gets. But not this time, not with Derek, and that failure must surely eat at him.

Tarja proved as independent in marriage to Derek as she'd ever been with Scarbrough. Dragging her lesbian model lover to Nepal was only the tail end of several affairs. She flew to Paris to tend to Rey when he relapsed into drug use, then flew to Rome where she was seen at a nightspot with Chirico. None of this was public prior to Derek's death.

Without her husband's knowledge, she also secured the contract from *Brides R Us* and for several days in Kathmandu posed for glamour shots. She was the woman who'd landed the world's most eligible and richest bachelor. Every woman wanted to imagine for a few moments that they were she.

Tarja gloried in the attention. You might say she was born to it, soaking it in like a dry sponge, lapping up every drop like a greedy cat, a sex kitten. Whenever a camera was pointed in her direction, she presented her dazzling smile for approval, much like a local television anchor. If she ever turned down an interview, no one's heard about it.

It is said that her husband was pleased with all the attention given to his new wife. If true, he didn't stay pleased for long.

Such was the interest in the Sodoc Foundation Everest expedition that once it reached Base Camp, it was besieged by media crews from Spain, Germany, France, United Kingdom, Russia, Korea, and many others—not counting the Italian and Japanese crews accompanying them on the trek. At Base Camp, these were there to cover climbers from their own nations for the most part, but the presence of the international darling newlyweds was irresistible.

This was to be Derek's conquest of the last of the Seven Summits and the final piece of a three-year effort. It had been a busy eighteen months—even apart from his quickie marriage. He'd climbed Aconcagua in Argentina, Vinson Massif in Antarctica, and Mt. Kilimanjaro in Kenya in rapid succession. Everest was the climax and SNS pitched the story relentlessly, working viewers into a fever pitch. The result was that the expedition more closely resembled a traveling circus than a serious climbing party.

First was affable Calvin Seavers, usually known simply as Doc. The two had known each other for years and were frequent climbing partners. Pals say the two were as bonded as lovers, though there was no suggestion of anything other than a close friendship. The year before Derek's triumph in Antarctica, Doc had been with him at Aconcagua in South America and restored him to health in the midst of a blizzard that claimed three lives.

Next was Scott Devlon, a friend of more recent vintage who had accompanied Derek and Doc on the conquest of Aconcagua. It is said that Derek particularly wanted Scott on this climb, for reasons never adequately explained. A decorated Afghanistan war hero, linguist, and professor, Scott appeared from all accounts delighted to be along.

Reggie Maul owned and operated one of the most successful Himalayan climbing companies. Maul had also been part of the South American climb; in that adventure the pair had formed a fast and lasting friendship based on a mutual love of mountains and trust. Derek placed his safety and life into the hands of the hearty New Zealander. Reggie was determined that nothing would happen to his friend—even at the cost of his own life.

Also with Derek was Peer Borgen, perhaps the world's most gifted Alpine climber. Brought aboard to enhance European ratings for the big show, he was also expected to help on the approaches of the mountain. Gregarious, courageous, and fun loving, he was considered by many the ideal climbing companion.

But there is more to his story—much more, if you believe certain Web sites and blogs. It is claimed (though not substantiated, it should be said) that Peer was paid an exorbitant sum to rekindle his long-dormant relationship with Tarja in order to break up the happy couple. It is said, though Peer vehemently denies it, that he was paid by none other than—you guessed it—Michael Sodoc.

And there was Crystal Hernandez, Derek's jilted lover, SNS producer, and an amateur climber herself. Who knows what thoughts and motives coursed through her hormone-driven body? She thought she'd landed Derek and then lost him to Tarja. The blow was a profound one, from all accounts and, by almost any standard, she had no business on the expedition. But Derek had faith in her and successfully covering his final triumph would have been a tremendous boost to her career—so there she was, rage and all.

Finally, there was Rusty Landon, Derek's cameraman. A skilled mountaineer, he was also a combat veteran of the first Gulf War and was allegedly angry that Derek had stolen Crystal from him months earlier, angrier that he'd dumped her so unceremoniously, and angriest that she'd not come crawling back.

Rusty deserves close scrutiny, for he has never been forthcoming about his role in the military. One source reports that he was in Special Forces—part of a deep desert penetration team where he served as a sniper. Another claims that he was attached to Delta Force as a freelance assassin. Still another insists he was assigned to the U. S. military, but was actually in the CIA and conducted special operations for them. Rusty has never publicly commented on any of these reports.

Each brought his or her own skill and talents to the expedition—along with considerable baggage of one kind or another. Of them all, only Reggie had climbed Everest previously. It was not intended that either Doc or Scott would summit and Rusty only as he filmed Derek. After all, the purpose of the expedition was to put Derek on the top of the world. But in the end, many were gripped with summit fever and, in the final hours of that disastrous day, as I discovered, they placed their own personal ambitions above any commitment to friendship.

In retrospect, it seems foolish for Derek to have surrounded himself with so many amateurs and untrustworthy professionals. It was an unsavory rat pack escorting him up that mountain—men and women consumed by motives and seeking objectives we can scarcely grasp, even now. Much of it was unknown to Derek, but he surely knew a great deal. Such was the measure of his hubris in his certainty that he believed he could not fail. He'd never failed previously, why should he now?

In their ignorance, though, all save Reggie and Peer were utterly unprepared for the reality they would face. Before this climb was completed, many of those on whom Derek relied would be dead. Limbs would be lost. Deceit would run amok. Reputations would lie in tatters—if they weren't already. As for Derek, he'd end up a frozen corpse near the summit of Everest.

—*vvvv*—

Every aspect of the expedition was meticulously planned. No expense had been spared. Every effort was made to reduce risk and see to comfort. Everything that could be controlled, was—or so Derek thought.

What Derek could not bend to his will was the weather, but in the beginning that seemed to make no difference. It was a delightful spring that year, all agree—one enjoyed by few expeditions in the long decades of Everest climbs. In such lovely circumstances, it was easy to see how the myth of Shangri-La was born. This time it served as a cover for what can only be accurately described as a den of iniquity.

After leaving the trucks and buses behind, the expedition advanced on foot through portions of Nepal that are absolutely stunning in their splendor. Every bit of arable land in that region is under cultivation. Hillsides are lovingly and gracefully terraced in exquisite winding rows. Below, stretches of brown and gray rock and dirt are interspersed with the verdant green of well-tended cultivated fields.

Accounts tell that as the expedition snaked its way through the foothills, it passed lovely fields of vivid grass and bright wild flowers. Sparkling streams of pure glacier water gurgled down from the lofty peaks. Laughing Sherpa children greeted the expedition, handing flowers to the climbers as they passed. No climbing expedition has ever had a more beautiful approach trek.

And everywhere were reminders of the region's Buddhist faith. Strings of prayer flags stretched across the hillsides, fluttering and snapping in the breeze. A rock prayer mound with strings of Buddhist prayer flags was in every pass that the expedition crossed. Daily, the Sherpa knelt in prayer.

Too bad everyone didn't join it. Who knows, the extra karma might have spared a few lives. That's what the Sherpa thought and whispered among themselves.

The approach to the mother of all mountains leads trekkers through an ancient kingdom, rich with tradition and a historical culture that Westerners are rapidly destroying, as evidenced by Derek's expedition and those leading or trailing it. This cult of the mountain has at its core an uncaring desire to debase what it does not understand, all in the childish pursuit of standing on the highest point on earth, to be king of the mountain if only for a few brief minutes.

On the far horizon, the mountain range stands remote and obscure. Only as you approach the immense peak do you realize its enormity. It makes any normal person seem puny, as nothing. It is with great excitement that you confront your destiny and begin the high adventure! So it is described by those who have been there and those who were with Derek that year—at least the ones who cared.

You are drawn by the ghosts of all the giants who have gone before you. Mallory, Irvine, Hillary, Tenzing! Their spirit calls out to you! You experience their presence every step of the trek, every inch of the trek! As it was for others, so it was for Derek and his band of adventurers.

Portions of Nepal inspired the novel, movie, and legend of Shangri-La—a valley paradise of peace, harmony, and plenty nestled within the Himalayas—a land where happy men and women live immortal lives in perfect tranquility.

The incredible beauty of this mystical land was marred only by the abject poverty and filth that the expedition encountered in every village and settlement along the route. The dirty-faced children ran laughing to greet the Westerners, their hands extended, looking for gifts of candy or money.

But looking beyond these experiences, with the frequent bubbling streams, spring showers, magnificent views, high snowcapped mountains, cascading waterfalls, and invigorating air, it is no wonder that this region was selected for the hidden valley of Shangri-La. Few places on earth possess such magnificent natural beauty.

But Nepal is no mythical kingdom and the foothills of the Himalayas are not Shangri-La. It is a bitter, cold place with death serving as the ultimate reality.

# Why Derek Climbs

*By Frederick G. Collins*
*World News Syndicate*
*May 13*

If all goes as planned, and when it comes to Derek Sodoc it usually does, the self-described adventurer will stand astride the tallest point on earth sometime over the next three weeks. Earlier this month, he set out to conquer Everest leading the most lavish, as well as one of the largest, expeditions in recent decades.

The younger Mr. Sodoc, only son of powerful world media tycoon Michael Sodoc, could have selected the easy path of following in his father's footsteps. Instead, he turned his back on that obvious career choice, electing instead to pursue his own path. Since breaking out on his own, Derek Sodoc has launched his own syndicated outdoor television series, produced and narrated six documentaries, and climbed the tallest mountains on six of the world's continents. With the conquest of Everest, he'll bag all seven.

So why does he do it? Climbing at these altitudes is grueling, demanding—not to mention dangerous—work. As many as a dozen climbers perish on the summit of Everest every year.

"He does it to prove he's his own man," Rex Winter, author of *My Life, My Career,* wrote. "He refuses to live in his father's shadow."

Others say that there is more to it. "He genuinely loves the challenge. Even with all the technological improvements in climbing gear, every summit attempt is demanding, and for that reason intensely satisfying," said one of his closest friends recently.

Jane Litter has served as publicist on Sodoc's most recent climbs and offered her perspective. "In this modern world, as we trash our planet and destroy the environment, these expeditions provide climbers with a chance to enjoy nature in these remote locales, before it too is destroyed."

# Chapter Three

# Into the Abyss

From all accounts, this was a transitional phase for the new marriage. The actions of the young couple certainly support that opinion. This was not unexpected. All marriages have their adjustment phase shortly after the thrill of the wedding and honeymoon. As the excitement diminishes and expectations are reconsidered, reality sets in. For most, this is nothing more than a less smooth time in the relationship as they get on with the business of life as a couple.

But for Derek and Tarja, there'd been one adventure after another—from the moment they met until the day Tarja became a widow. There was no period of quiet, no time of introspection, no meaningful emotional interaction to serve as an anchor for the future. Despite their personal failings and indiscretions, they lived a sort of fairy-tale existence, traveling the globe in their self-imposed opulent cocoon.

Derek spent much of that time preoccupied with last-minute preparations for the doomed expedition. Certainly this was of necessity, but perhaps he was also escaping the hasty decision he'd made. Subtracting their two-week honeymoon on

Bora Bora, Derek had just ten weeks for the final details. Who knows how much of that time was filled with the necessities of a new husband? Or how much that contributed to his demise?

Tarja certainly made good use of those weeks. In addition to finding time for her model lover, she hired a new, more aggressive publicist, recruited a make-up and hair stylist to join her on the expedition, and closed the lucrative deal with *Brides R Us* magazine. Rumor has it that she was to have become a regular columnist with the rag and planned to shop her ghostwritten pieces to newspapers. We'll never know for certain—and that's certainly no loss.

There was initially no sign of matrimonial trouble on the trek. It may be that Derek had not heard of the hot model who'd entertained Tarja before his arrival or perhaps he didn't care. Many men do not consider a lesbian relationship to be infidelity and are, in fact, excited by the thought, regretting only that they weren't invited along for the ride.

Derek and Tarja were inseparable—at night and by day. Pals say they appeared happy enough, ducking into their spacious tent at odd hours, the young bride giggling if not exactly blushing.

"Seeing them together was like watching Hollywood movie stars. They radiated magnetism. Together it was increased by a factor of four. You could get sunburned standing too close to them," one source on the expedition wrote in an article.

Tarja Sodoc was certainly an odd bride—perhaps one of the oddest in history—and that excludes her peccadilloes. Preoccupied with her looks, behaving daily as a *prima donna*, she demanded camera time. Whenever the great adventurer gave an interview, Tarja could be counted on to hang on his arm, her chest jutting to maximum, a come-hither look in her misty eyes as she worshiped the camera lens. If Tarja had a love affair beyond herself, it can surely be said it was with the camera.

Despite all the sexual energy generated along the trail, the bloom was definitely off the rose and the honeymoon was over—dead, dead, dead—before the couple ever reached Base Camp, well before either so much as set a foot on the mountain itself. The couple was seen standing apart from the rest, engaged in deep, heated conversations, Tarja clearly wanting her way, Derek unwilling to give it.

"For one thing, Derek was very angry about her piggybacking an expansion of her career onto his. He'd thought all that settled before they married. Now she was breaking the deal," a knowledgeable insider says. "The brilliant light of publicity was to be directed solely at him, not diverted to her. Let her build her own career, not steal a portion of his. It was a message he understood, one she ignored. And the stories of her misbehavior had surely reached him by this time. We all knew; surely he did as well."

Others disagree. "The man knew nothing. She had him so loaded up on dope he was in his own world."

The other climbers clearly loved being on the expedition. Jocular Doc smiled as he went about repairing tired and injured feet, dispensing much-appreciated pills, and later administering essential shots. Crystal vamped her way up the trail, initially flirting outrageously with an Italian cameraman, publicly primping before the mirror attached to the forward pole of her tent before trotting off to spend the night with him—and later with others.

"She was quite a lady," Umberto Prodi says. "The last thing I expected—even as an Italian—was for there to be so much sex on Everest. It came as a real shock. Crystal was fun, but not like you think. She'd been hurt—even I could see that. It was revenge sex. She flaunted it afterward. I suppose if I'd cared, I could have figured out who she wanted to make jealous—but I didn't care. It only happened a few times, then she moved on. Me? I had my eye on this little Jap girl."

Rusty, Crystal's former paramour, was a sulking observer, kept busy by Crystal filming the expedition and recording interviews with Derek at every opportunity. Who knows what he was really thinking? Anger seemed to lurk just beneath his surface and his sullen mood disturbed more than one. "He was an odd duck, I'll say that much," one of the climbers told me in confidence. "I wouldn't have wanted to climb alone with him. Or to have angered him in camp."

Peer, the magnificent Norwegian climbing superstar, gloried in the attention of the European media, but beyond that was available at every water crossing, prepared to do what was necessary for the slippery-footed, of whom there were several. Once the expedition reached snow, he began training the less skilled to help them accomplish a safe summit. Few in history in such a situation were as unselfish and devoted to others as Peer was. He was in every way a modern-day George Mallory.

En route up the lovely climbing slopes toward Base Camp, from where the real climbing began, Derek was filmed or gave an interview at every stop. This did not include the staged sections of him trekking beside a yak or Sherpa. When the others rested or sought diversion, Derek worked. Observers say that someone had a piece of him every waking hour. At one stop, it was Crystal and Rusty, the next it would be an interview with the Italian or Japanese film crews or one of the others.

Not that he minded. In the short decades of his life, he was one of those people who thrived in the intense spotlight of attention. In fact, whenever the camera turned away—say toward his greedy, lovely wife—Derek seemed to fade a bit, to become a pale mirage of his usual self.

At night, Derek worked with his producer recording voiceovers, screening the recordings from that day, selecting what would be used and what would be discarded. The media tent glowed a metallic white late into the night. The consequence of all this hard work and dedication was that nearly every day pieces were uploaded and dispatched to New York for airing. SNS prospered from it, while we can only speculate what toll it extracted from Derek.

It's been said that to a teenage boy a car is a bedroom on wheels. It can honestly be said that this expedition was a traveling bedroom—or rather a mobile tent city of bedrooms. The simple Sherpa played their part, as they are not known for their dedication to one woman. In fact, a well-paid guide will usually acquire several wives. Away from their village, they'll have sex with any woman they can pay or talk into it. It is their way of life and who's to judge? They have few pleasures in their short lives.

On the trek, men Sherpa outnumbered the women by five to one. Two of the women were with their husbands, who kept a close eye on them. The other three were without men, though not without their frequent company. Their Eastern culture has standards that are alien to our own. When it came to sex, the Sherpa, both men and women, live different lives and conduct themselves with different standards. Two of the remaining three women behaved no differently than most of the Western women climbers did. They had a few lovers along the way, but nothing serious.

However, one was very different. Unlike the other women, who were weather-beaten and aged beyond their years, she was attractive. Lighthearted and bubbly, she was also an easy conquest—if such a word applies to a woman who gives herself so readily. It was understood that a bauble or two—even some money was necessary—but most of all, a man need do nothing more than ask politely.

This should have been no problem—and for the first week it was not. Then the first symptoms appeared. The woman had contracted a venereal disease before setting out and was spreading a nasty form of gonorrhea with every encounter. Doc was busy giving shots left and right, but the infection persisted.

It would disappear for a week or two and then return. Doc Calvin was never able to stamp it out entirely.

At first, the pestilence was limited to the Sherpa. But that would change, disastrously so.

---

Venereal disease wasn't the only specter to stalk the expeditions. The Italian team was especially hard struck by a persistent bug that produced fevers and diarrhea. "It was inexplicable," Benito Luci, the team leader, told a reporter on his return. "No one else suffered from it as we did. Only us. We were suspicious from the first. When it persisted, I ordered a watch on our food supplies and preparation. The bug would leave us then, but at the first lax occasion it returned. I'm convinced we were sabotaged. Someone wanted us to turn back. I know it."

One of the Italian climbers, in fact, became so ill he was forced to give up. The team was delayed two days as they nursed him. Once he was on his way back, the Italians pressed hard to catch up with the Sodoc expedition.

Among the Westerners, sexual liaisons continued, oblivious to what the Sherpa were about. Crystal slept her way around once she lost interest in the Italian; Rusty was no monk, from accounts; Peer was much sought after and not one to say no. The nearby teams bed-hopped nearly every night. On the approach, climbers were at least as preoccupied with coupling as they were with trekking.

For a time, though, it didn't seem to matter. These were, after all, sophisticated adults. Everyone understood. No harm, no foul.

---

Each day of the approach march, that mighty peak loomed nearer and nearer. The mountain could not be ignored as it grew in time to dominate every vista. A sense of excitement and febrile anticipation pervaded the expedition; every eye turned to the massive pyramid towering above. The sensation experienced by all is best described is a sort of fever, an ardor that slowly enveloped all the climbers. As the expedition neared Base Camp, those there say that every climber was talking as if summiting was a certainty.

Seasoned guide Gyurme was head of the Sherpa. Short and sturdy, dogged and determined, he possessed the kind of leadership and prerequisite climbing skill essential to leading that hearty race. From every account, he performed magnificently and did a very efficient job on the way to Base Camp where his luck ran out or his fate was fulfilled—depending on your interpretation.

The Sherpa porters, herders, and climbing guides were oblivious to the Peyton Place they had joined—or perhaps not so much oblivious as amused by it. Westerners routinely travel to Asia to behave strangely without the usual controls on their behavior; these were no different, though it has been noted that climbers typically conducted themselves with greater comportment and dignity. One can only wonder if Derek, de facto leader of the expedition, really grasped the nature of what was taking place right beneath his nose. Or did the distractions of his work and the demands of his needy wife, diffuse his focus and divert his attention from matters he should have known about?

Or perhaps there were other reasons why he did nothing.

Derek enjoyed the kind of life every man dreams about—a sort of James Bondish existence without being shot at. He lived where he wanted, at exotic locations, in incredible luxury, traveled where and how he wanted, and died as one of the most famous people in the world.

Along the way, he never lacked for feminine companionship, bedding desirable women at will. Most of the world's beauties, from movie stars to models, had been on his arm at one time or another. Three years earlier, it had been rumored that the heir to the Danish throne wanted to marry the dashing adventurer. He could have had any woman he desired and certainly had his share, but for reasons known only to him, he wanted Tarja. Like the portrait of Dorian Gray, her beauty was skin deep; the ugly depths of her depravity concealed within her soul, hidden beneath that glorious facade.

Even though the South Pole is perhaps the most remote and desolate place on earth, the highest point on Antarctica is not especially demanding as mountains go. It is ironic, in fact, that most of the Seven Summits are not all that difficult to climb. Even Everest, the widow-maker, requires little technical skill. The challenge is its location and extreme elevation.

Vinson Massif stands at just 16,067 feet. It is climbed in the Antarctic summer and, though there is continuous daylight at that time of year, the temperatures linger at minus 20 degrees Fahrenheit. The mountain is accessed by first flying to Punta Arenas, Chile, the world's southernmost large city with a population in excess of 100,000. Windy and cool even in summer, it is a smaller version of San Francisco and well off the beaten path. A commercial fishing center, local restaurants serve some of the finest fish dishes in the world. The people live uncomplicated lives, apart from most of the world, separate even from most of Chile.

Vinson Massif is reached after a six-hour flight from Punta Arenas aboard a Russian IL-76 to the Blue Ice Runway at Patriot Hills. There, climbers switch to a Twin Otter that transports them to Base Camp. No trekking here. No weeks spent roughing it. No sir. Not if you have the money. There are typically two additional camps on the approach and, in most cases, from Chile to the peak and back takes a mere two weeks, weather permitting. A cakewalk for any climber of experience.

Derek had already climbed four of the highest mountains when he and his small entourage arrived at Cabo de Hornos, a European-style hotel in the heart of Punta Arenas beside the traditional main plaza. It was presumably a coincidence that Tarja was staying there as well.

Or perhaps not.

Pals say Derek and Tarja met at the Cabo de Hornos bar. The attraction was immediate and mutual. Both were to leave the next day for the Antarctic Base Camp, but weather kept them warm and cozy at the resort hotel, dividing their time between the bar and bedroom. By the time the weather cleared, Derek emerged looking as if he'd been drained of every ounce of energy. Tarja, in comparison, positively glowed.

The following week, they summited the spectacular peak with its majestic view of ice and snow. From South America, they immediately jetted to Africa, where they toured the Serengeti Riff and then climbed Mt. Kilimanjaro together. Very romantic. They were wed a few days later off Mauritius on the yacht of the Sultan of Brunei and promptly flew to Bora Bora for their exotic honeymoon.

None of this, of course, was the coincidence Tarja conspired to make it appear. Since her unceremonious departure from Manhattan, she'd born a deep, abiding grudge. It wasn't Scarbrough's rejection that stung; he'd served her purpose and she'd been well paid for her time with him. No, it was Michael Sodoc casting her off like a used coat. Close friends say she chafed at the humiliation and that she vowed revenge.

"Sodoc was her target. A powerful media mogul, no other man in the world was better positioned to make her the mega-celebrity she lusted to be. Even his new Russian bride was no obstacle. But he was a shrewd man, and women like Tarja were a dime a dozen in his life. She was nothing to him—and that's what hurt most of all," says a former hairdresser who knows everything and shares not the confessional seal of secrecy.

When exactly Tarja fixed on Derek no one knows, and it is possible, though unlikely, that this part might actually have been serendipity. Once she began her conquest of the Seven Summits, it was inevitable that the pair would encounter one another at some point. Perhaps that's why she picked the mountains. Unlike the Kennedy clan, it was not the custom of the senior Sodoc to share his mistresses with his son. It is possible, likely even, that Derek had no idea that Tarja and his father had even slept together.

But Tarja knew and she understood that Derek was off limits. Or should have been.

Her meeting him in Chile was no accident, a pal says. "She knew he was going there. She arranged to arrive first. It was planned. Even the wedding. She ordered the dress as soon as she came back from Antarctica—even before they left for Africa. She knew what she was after and got it. Revenge."

All the while, according to reports, upon learning what was taking place beyond his control, Michael Sodoc raged in his Manhattan penthouse/office. Hearing his only son was traveling with Tarja in Africa, he immediately called Derek. The conversation went nowhere. In fact, it may very well have pushed Derek in the direction Sodoc most dreaded.

Realizing what he was up to, Sodoc dispatched a close confidant, Tom Bauman, in an attempt to talk sense to his son—but by the time Bauman arrived, the couple was wed. From that day until the one when his son died, the senior Sodoc worked to have the marriage annulled.

Friends say there may be another side to this story. In a quiet corner bar in Manhattan, a once-close Derek confidant told me, "Derek knew about Tarja and his father. He knew. He wanted to see what she was like, what all the buzz was about. Then he called me from Chile. He was drunk. He said he had the most wonderful idea. He'd marry the bitch—that's what he called her, the 'bitch'—and really stick it to his old man. You've got part of it right. It was about revenge. You've just got the wrong player."

Tarja had struck gold, in every way. She managed to marry Derek without a prenuptial agreement. Upon her husband's death, she stood to inherit hundreds of millions. Should Sodoc have died first, then Derek after him, she'd have received billions and worldwide control of SNS. This because the Russian bride is locked into an unbreakable prenuptial. In the event of neither, in the case of a divorce, Tarja could have threatened the Sodoc family control of their global media enterprise.

The marriage came as a shock to more than the groom's father and pregnant Russian stepmother. Neither of Tarja's parents were informed or invited to the wedding. Yet within the week, a careful post-wedding picture appeared on the covers of *People* and *Hello!* magazines.

---

In the most significant way, however, the true romance was over by the time the newlyweds gathered in Nepal. It was apparent to anyone with eyes, almost from the start. Tarja's obsession with piggybacking her fame on Derek's back stood in stark contrast to what should have been her true role as a loyal wife. Climbers report frequent disagreements between the couple, followed by passionate reconciliations, though they say the reconciliations became less and less frequent and increasingly less passionate.

Nevertheless, Tarja's desire to enhance her tarnished public image at her husband's expense was not the fundamental problem. He surely knew that she wanted to be in the public eye. She'd certainly worked hard enough at it. Had she been more discreet, less greedy, less rushed, her lust for celebrity might very well have been no problem at all. Some men like being known to have sex with a woman that others desire. That may very well have been Tarja's appeal to him.

No, that alone was not enough. There was something else, a snake in this garden.

It came as no surprise to those who knew Derek that marriage did nothing to end his wandering eye and single-minded conquest of more-than-willing women. Derek was the kind of man who cheated even when he was happily married. We've all known them, men who cheat relentlessly on a perfectly attractive and decent wife, become morose when she leaves them, and then pursue a younger clone of the first wife relentlessly—and once remarried, proceed to cheat shamelessly. For them, the wedding ring is their aphrodisiac.

Within weeks of taking his wedding vows, Derek began a passionate affair with Crystal in New York City while he planned the coverage of the expedition. The pair was inseparable. "They went at it hot and heavy," a pal said. "They couldn't keep their hands off each other."

Crystal, daughter of Cuban immigrants, is a hotheaded Latin beauty and, from all accounts, took her relationship with Derek more seriously than he did. "She was in love," a source says. "He was her one and only. She fell for him in a way she never had for anyone else, and that includes Rusty. She walked around six inches in the air, that sickening rosy glow all over her. Friends tried to warn her, but she wouldn't listen." She was talking about marriage—even though he'd already married Tarja.

"Crystal was stunned and humiliated when Derek dropped her," a source told me. "It seemed to her that everywhere she went people in the know were laughing at her."

But Crystal was not unique. In most ways, Derek was more a man's man than one on whom a woman could depend. Women served one important purpose in his life; with the exception of climbing mountains, the conquest of every reasonably attractive female within striking distance was his relentless goal.

This kind of implacable womanizing among the famous is standard fare and a bit pathetic—though most would say not in Derek's case. He accepted the occasional rebuke with good cheer and never bragged of his conquests to his friends.

And it should be said in all fairness that Derek did little pursuing. Women threw themselves at him wherever he went. Even with his lovely bride by his side, beautiful women pressed themselves against him, slipped bits of paper with their telephone numbers into his hand, and whispered endearments into his ear. He accepted the attention with a sense of entitlement and good humor.

But in this regard, Tarja had no sense of humor. More than once, she shouted at women to get away from her husband, allegedly coming to blows in public twice. Derek took it all as great fun, which only angered Tarja further.

So it was that the couple's troubles were well developed by the time they arrived in Nepal. It may be that Tarja had learned of his earlier affair with Crystal and that might well be why she arrived with a girlfriend. They'd certainly not been discreet and there was always someone willing to tattle. But for Derek it didn't end with the high-spirited Cubana. One member of the expedition reported seeing Derek emerge from a hotel room of an SNS international producer—not Crystal's.

"She was hot, no question about it," the source says. "She'd been chasing him relentlessly for days. That guy had all the luck—until the end, of course."

Another relates witnessing the early portion of the night Derek spent with a member of the Nepalese Royal family at the palace. "I thought they'd kill him for that. The Royal family in Nepal is sacred. If they fool around, it is with their own—not with outsiders and certainly not with a Western man. But he got away with it," a source says. "She was calling him incessantly after that. He told me that royal pussy was no different than the regular stuff."

There are other stories and rumors of liaisons even before the expedition left Kathmandu. Not all of them were high-class, either. Derek liked to rut with the best of them. Given his reputation, it is easy to believe every story—and we likely don't even know the half of it.

These liaisons were reasonably circumspect and it is believed that Tarja was unaware of them or at least was able to turn a blind eye. To some observers, his behavior was shocking. Why would a man so recently married and to such a well-known beauty want to cheat so openly and frequently?

"I think Derek liked the forbidden. He enjoyed sleazy women; we all knew that. He'd had a close call more than once because of it. Frankly, he preferred raunch to propriety. I don't think Tarja was enough of a slut to satisfy him—and that's saying a lot," a pal says. "If he'd known her better, things might have had a very different ending. The only real mistake she made with that black model was not asking Derek to join in."

These ready conquests continued for Derek on the trek to Base Camp. There was, as if another example is needed, the incident with Sabrina Bellucci, the producer with the Italian film crew. "I could tell he wanted me," she told an Italian magazine later. "I can always tell. Any woman can, for that matter. I wanted more access and I found him attractive. What could be more natural? It all went well, but his producer refused to let me interview him. Still, when he could, he came back. I'm not one for those quick American things, you know, and he was a lusty man. What else could I do?"

Word inevitably spread through the expedition that Derek was up to his usual tricks. Who can say when Tarja learned the truth? A husband is typically the last to know when his wife has an affair; perhaps the reverse is true of a wife when her husband is having multiple affairs. Maybe she really didn't know, perhaps she pretended it wasn't going on. It's more likely that she didn't want to know. It is even more likely that when she did hear of it, she could not believe it—despite her own behavior.

What kind of man would treat her like that? Worse, what would people think? Her face and figure had graced the covers of a hundred magazines. She was a sought-after beauty who associated with—and had been pursued by—the richest and most desirable men in world. She had her own rutting pack and had picked Derek to receive her favors. How could the man she'd selected treat her like this?

Surely she found it incomprehensible, especially given her arrogance and pride. The easiest course of action was to deny what was going on. So while friends and other men could understand what Derek was up to and accept it—that was not the case with his wife once the reality was thrust into her face. To her, it was an egregious wrong and quite literally, when the time came, there would be hell to pay.

But first it was necessary that she debase herself. As Tarja's suspicions were heightened while he was visiting Sabrina, she became what the Chinese call Mrs. Follower. She took to tagging after her husband wherever he went. No longer was he given any independence. "I was keeping that wop whore away," she told her hairdresser. She sat in on every meeting, was present at every discussion, and stayed within arm's length of him at all hours of the day or night. He didn't like it, that was clear, but nothing he could say kept her away. Her behavior was a source of amusement to the others; Derek found nothing funny about it at all.

But the reality of the trek to Everest is that it was impossible for her to always be with him.

―――

In the first decades that climbers assaulted Everest, they did so with the honor that has historically accompanied such efforts. Teams helped one another; supplies were stashed at advanced camps with no concern for safety. After all, who would steal? All that has changed in recent years.

Now large teams employ professional guards or assign guides to guard duty to protect supplies of every kind. At first, thefts of supplies were limited to the Nepalese guides. If they needed crampons, they might steal a pair for use, knowing a Western climber always had a spare. Perhaps they'd help themselves to thermal underwear or high-altitude socks.

A Nepalese expedition comprised primarily of university students which trekked immediately in front of the Sodoc expedition was suspected in the thefts. Girija Dahal gave an interview after the disaster and said, "It was easy to blame us. Our team was most respectable and in no way participated in any theft. I admit not liking Mr. Sodoc as I thought his behavior toward our goddess was inexcusable, but we played no part in the sabotage. I am, in fact, offended at the suggestion."

By the time of the Sodoc expedition, foodstuffs, medicine, boots, clothing, anything and everything were routinely stolen. Supplies left at the advanced camps had to be guarded, adding to the cost and size of expeditions. Some items were stolen to be sold, others to be used.

Even that is not all. Teams in competition now use theft as a form of sabotage. Deny another team vital communication equipment, or enough climbing rope, or vital medicine, and you end its chances. In addition to disease, the white man has brought avarice. Nothing is sacred on Everest any longer.

—~~~—

Television reporter Reiki Nadasaka was twenty-seven years old that season. With better than average looks, she'd struggled to make it in the male-dominated Japanese media world. "You cannot imagine the kind of sexual harassment we Japanese women must endure to have any kind of a career," she told me over drinks. "Japan is very much a man's world."

A graduate of the prestigious University of Tokyo, where the elite of Japan have been trained for generations, she found her career stalled at the Nippon News Agency, despite several years of hard work. "My boss made it clear he wanted to sleep with me," she said in our exclusive interview. *"Baka ka!* Asshole. He was married so I thought it would be safe. I wasn't looking for a husband, or even a long-term relationship, just a way to get out of the cutting room where I was trapped. I'm not proud of it, but others have done the same, even men I know for a fact that are not gay, and I'm no better than them."

The lovely Reiki then recounts her horrendous ordeal in the hands of a man she candidly calls "a pervert." She goes on, "I don't know what to call the things he wanted me to do, *chikusho* f**k, but I don't consider them to be sex. I was in counseling for months afterward, until the counselor tried to sleep with me as well. It was no wonder my boss had to exploit vulnerable young women like me to fulfill his lust."

When she refused to submit any longer, Reiki found herself assigned to the Sodoc Everest expedition, given greater duties than she was prepared for, and provided with no time to train. "He wanted an excuse to fire me, but I refused to let him succeed. It wasn't easy, but I kept up with everyone and filed excellent stories from the trek before we were forced to turn back."

Also present on the Japanese expedition was Fuyuto Kirosaki, at one time Reiki's fiancé and also an employee of Nippon News Agency. "He was a drunk," she told me a bit defensively. "He used to beat me. What a real *teme,* son of a b***h. Really! I'm not making this up. And he was jealous of any man who even looked at me. He was sent along at the last minute to make my life hell, to get me to change my mind. But it didn't work."

Others see it differently. "She wasn't qualified for the work she did. She expected the rest of us to pick up her load. She was sleeping with her boss, and that's how she got the assignment. She arrived in Kathmandu completely ill equipped. We had to go out and find everything she'd need there. She thought her good looks made everything possible. It was hell working with her. Once we were on the hike to the mountain, she complained about everything: the dirt, sore feet, and the food. It was miserable to be around her."

Asked about Fuyuto, the source told me, "He was all right with her. He'd stopped drinking. I think she drove him back to it. She almost had me drinking. He told me he thought their boss had sent him along as a joke. She used to tease him. She'd flash her naked body at him. I saw her rolling her tongue across her lips once, taunting him. A real *yariman*, slut. And when she did have sex with one of us, she always made sure he knew. He was only flesh and blood. It was bound to turn out badly. You know women—they cannot help but be trouble. And, frankly, she wasn't all that good. Certainly not worth all the trouble she caused."

At first, when Derek allowed her to film him, Reiki thought she'd scored a coup. She walked around the small Japanese campsite bragging she'd bagged the "big one." But then Derek let himself be filmed by the Italians and others as well, and she realized she'd gotten nothing special.

"But he gave no one a personal interview," the source says. "Those he saved for SNS. Once she figured that out, Reiki was determined more than ever to get one."

The way the petite beauty went about it was obvious to everyone. "She was going to screw him to get it. She thought the campaign went well when she first caught his eye, but that blonde wife of his was having none of it. She'd been having trouble with that Italian. She ran Reiki off with a rock. But Reiki was nothing if not relentless. Tarja couldn't be everywhere all the time—and she had the Italian to worry about."

The source says Reiki gave Derek the eye and he knew what that was all about. One night when he was left alone for twenty minutes, he went to her tent. Anyone passing by could figure out what happened after that. "From all the noise in there, the way he grunted and groaned, I'd say she gave him a pretty good time," the source said. "Better than I ever got out of her, but then I'm not a billionaire. She got the warm-jelly crotch-lock on him and really made him howl. But one trip up her velvet freeway wasn't enough to change his regular road map. A couple more detours might have done the job. After all, she had some tricks that would make a dead pony whinny. But when Derek came out of the tent there was Fuyuto, drunker than hell."

This and a subsequent confrontation have been well covered in several magazine articles. Fuyuto, reeling about as if he were trying to keep his balance on a ship's deck in a storm, shouted at Derek. "She's my woman! What you doing with her?" He waved a bottle of sake over his head. It wasn't clear whether he intended to throw the bottle or stagger close enough to Derek to brain him with the booze. In any case, Fuyuto was so furious that he obviously didn't care whether he wasted the rest of the intoxicant. A dangerous attitude.

"Take it easy," Derek said, easing away. "We were just discussing an interview. She gets into that stuff pretty deep. You know that."

Then Reiki came out, clutching an REI fleece shirt to her bare chest. "Fuyuto! What are you doing here? Get away! Get away from here!"

The two argued in Japanese as a circle of men formed to watch. She slapped Fuyuto and the bottle fell out of his hand. It fractured on the rocks, spraying bits of glass and—more important to Fuyuto—sake. He looked stunned for a moment, an expression of loss arching his mouth and dampening his eyes. Whether he was mourning the end of the sake or his relationship with Reiki wasn't clear. Then his right hand snapped upward and lashed out. He caught her full on the left cheek, the blow landing with a harsh pop. She went backward suddenly across the snow, trying to find her balance, and dropped the fleece shirt, revealing the treasures the men were struggling over. Derek, whose romp in the treasure chest had left him fatigued—and who now was spooked by the crazy-faced Fuyuto—decided he wanted no part of this. His decision was reinforced by the sight of Tarja coming at him with bad juju contorting her face. He walked off hurriedly as Fuyuto shouted after him in English, "I will kill you, *gaijin*! You hear me? I will kill you!"

# Kickbacks Impoverish Sherpa

By Thakchay Topkay
*Kathmandu Times*
*May 21*

Everest climbing expeditions are required to pay off government officials in Nepal to avoid "trouble," reliable sources report.

"It's a disgrace," said Mr. Prosad Yadav in comments exclusive to the Kathmandu Times. "Besides contributing to a culture of corruption, it bleeds money from expeditions that would otherwise go to the Sherpa they employ thus contributing to their abject poverty."

Mr. Yadav, formerly a member of the National Council, called for a government crackdown on the abuses. According to reports, expeditions are routinely compelled to make cash payments to government officials to obtain permits for even the most basic supplies they must import to support their climb. Payments can be in the tens of thousands of rupees.

The Sherpa, who have cornered the market as Himalayan guides, are among the poorest ethnic groups in Nepal. They rely heavily on the fees their porters are paid to support the community. "The average income for a Sherpa porter has fallen by 20% in the last five years," Mr. Yadav said. "The money is finding its way into the pockets of corrupt officials."

Mr. Yadav recently announced his candidacy for leader of the Nepalese National Party.

# Chapter Four

# Fun and Games

Despite these problems, the weeks-long hike to Base Camp was in many ways a pleasant experience for most of the climbers. The scenery was glorious. Picturesque mountain peaks came daily into view; meadows of fragrant flowers were common in the lower elevations along with blooming plants of all kinds, while gardens of rock appeared above. A scented breeze drifted down from the valleys while the many streams bubbled with pristine water.

At night, the climbers gathered about several fires prepared by the Sherpa to swap stories and tell jokes. There was much laughter and gaiety. Occasionally one ducked off into the darkness, only to return in a bit with a grin as he buckled his pants. Derek can be best described as the social ringmaster of this traveling circus. He made it his purpose for everyone to enjoy themselves.

A form of pyrexia slowly gripped the camp. The ever-present mountain, the constant talk, the isolation, all led to the same thing—summit fever. Everyone wanted to reach the summit, to grab the brass ring, to get that photograph taken.

Historically, Everest has been conquered by friends. And when those climbing scarcely knew one another at departure, by summit day they were fast friends. But this wasn't just any expedition and no one on it became friends—unless you count sleeping-bag partners!

There has been much speculation about what happened to this doomed expedition. Numerous articles have been written on the subject and at least two television specials have aired, but none of them has touched on the real issue, the troubles that led inexorably to disaster. There has been talk of equipment theft and failures, especially of the digital radios. Speculation as well about the guides—claims that, for once, the Sherpa failed in their duty. There has also been talk about drug use and that Derek was too distracted by all the media and the relentless demands on his time and attention, that the dual purpose of the climb—reaching the summit while recording for his show—was beyond his capability and that of his team.

There is likely some truth to all of these, but none of them is on point. Derek and the others died because of sex. That's right. Good old-fashioned s-e-x. As you will see.

As it developed, Fuyuto refused to forget about Derek. After whacking Reiki, he knelt at her feet and sobbed, begging her to forgive him. "I don't excuse Fuyuto—even though that woman could drive any man to beat her," one of the Japanese crew told me. "But Reiki didn't handle it very well. One minute she was trying to calm the man down, next she was taunting him, calling him—well, I can only express it in American—a 'dickless wonder.' Fuyuto just went crazy, sobbing, ripping out tufts of his hair, the whole thing. He was her slave and now he knew his sex mistress was passing her ass around. You had to feel sorry for him. Of course, Derek wasn't her first little adventure. I'd had her. I think all of us did at one time or another. But to Fuyuto, she was the Virgin Mary—or at least she had been before Derek crawled up her leg."

Fuyuto resumed drinking heavily. The crew discussed trying to force him to go back down, but no one could figure out how to do it. Then a few days after Fuyuto discovered Derek outside Reiki's tent, he stomped into the Sodoc camp shortly after sunset, brandishing a Ginsu knife he'd taken from his team's cook. He confronted a reclining Derek. The knife flashed in the air, drawing patterns of elaborate dismemberment. "I'm going to kill you!" Fuyuto shouted, trying to keep his feet steady. Once again, he had a load of booze on and his feet wouldn't behave.

Peer stepped in front of the knife-wielder as Derek scrambled to his feet. "Hey, Fuyuto, the food's bad enough around here without stealing cookie's knives," Peer joked. "You need to get that thing back where it belongs right away. I'm starving."

Fuyuto was having none of that. "He f**ked her, he f**ked my Reiki!" he snarled. "I'm going to cut his nuts off—that's what I'm going to do. Get out of the way."

Peer stood his ground, looking for a chance to make a move for the knife. Derek continued to skulk behind him, his eyes roaming around looking for a way out. He obviously was going to leave the heavy lifting to Peer. That's the rich man's privilege, after all—let the cannon fodder get chewed up and don't put yourself on the line.

Peer had set himself up for a bad slashing or worse. All he had going for him, really, was his native wit: in the small space, there was no room to maneuver. "Tell you what," he said to Fuyuto, "I'll help you cut his nuts off. Actually, I've been cutting his nuts off behind his back anyway. Where do you think his wife goes when his climbing-rope goes limp?" The big Norwegian pounded his chest and laughed as if his lungs would burst.

Fuyuto hesitated, confused, and his moment of doubt was just enough. The tent flap snapped back, and two men from the Japanese team rushed through. One jumped on Fuyuto's back and drove him down; the other locked the elbow of his knife arm and twisted hard. The knife fell, pinged off a crampon that was lying on the ground, and skittered away. Then each seized an arm and pinioned Fuyuto.

"Sorry," the older of the two said, bowing slightly. In an instant, the tent-flap quivered again and all three men were gone.

"What was that about?" Tarja demanded, glaring at Peer and Derek.

"Just telling a big lie to get out of a tough situation," Peer replied.

Derek tried to walk away, but Tarja wasn't finished. "And what did you get from that juice-head's wife?" she asked her husband. The two went at it for more than an hour. By the time Reiki arrived at the Sodoc camp, Tarja had pulled the truth out of him.

Catfight alert! Tarja and Reiki had a go at each other that made the knife scene look tame. To tell the truth, having these two hot women getting it on was quite a treat for the male onlookers.

"You slut! Stay away from my husband!" Tarja shouted, giving Reiki a shove that almost put her on her back.

Reiki righted herself and put on an innocent, injured face. "Are you nuts?" she said. "What are you getting after me for? I didn't do anything. I just came to see if Derek was all right." She put out a hand to Derek, as if seeking assurance, but her eyes stayed on Tarja, who was huffing hard and showing her teeth.

"Derek, are you okay?" Reiki asked. "Did he hurt you?"

Tarja grabbed her jacket and jerked her away. "Don't talk to him! Get your yellow ass back to your own camp!"

"Racist bitch! If you ever make the Olympics, it will be as a member of the Swedish screwing team!"

"I'm American," Tarja reminded her.

"Then wrap the Stars and Stripes around your head and do it for Old Glory!" Reiki shot back. "You are past it, okay? You don't know anything." She looked at Derek. "We've got an interview scheduled." As Reiki said that, her look mixed fury with triumph. She hadn't meant to admit anything, but she clearly had.

Tarja blew. She grabbed Reiki's jacket again and shook the smaller woman like a captured rat. Then she stepped in close, released the grip of her right hand, and swung, overbalancing as she tried to punch Reiki in the forehead. The women teetered and then tumbled to the ground. For the next five minutes, the scene was all spit and screaming. A few strips of skin went elsewhere. Tarja absorbed a punch dangerously near her pleasure chamber, Reiki barely managed to get her left ear out of Tarja's grasp before she lost it entirely. Some very expensive climbing clothing wound up in rags. It was a holocaust in a teacup: sound and fury and lost dignity. One of the crew broke out his camera to film it. You can catch it on YouTube, though you can't tell it's Tarja from the angle.

Reiki told me breathlessly, "It wasn't my fault she couldn't keep her husband. He'd been after me for days. He really surprised me by showing up at my tent like that. I was bathing and he found me naked. He took that as a go-ahead sign, I guess. Anyway, he was cute and we were consenting adults. I must say the sex was very, very good. He was a real man, not like Japanese men at all. They're all just *yarichins*, sluts."

Derek stood aside, first looking bemused, then concerned as tufts of hair flew through the air. The fight went on for a good five minutes, until the women had run out of steam. Finally, he stepped in and broke the pair up.

"He led Tarja away," my source on the Japanese crew told me, "trying to calm her down. Reiki was furious. She had scratches on her face and her jacket was torn. She stomped around the campsite for a good ten minutes before calming down and returning to her own team."

———*ᴍᴍ*———

But it wasn't just women, no. In Kathmandu, Tarja had introduced Derek to a new, stronger form of hashish. After some time free of drugs, he found himself using heavily again. Tarja also had a supply of cocaine, which she began carefully feeding to him after her fight with the Japanese woman. Perhaps he took it initially to placate her. Who can say? Her plan, it seemed, was to use it to keep him under better control.

The effect was immediate and profound. Derek found it increasingly difficult to shoot his pieces or keep to any schedule. From all appearances, Tarja didn't care. She wanted him on a leash and was prepared to use whatever weapon she could find. She couldn't have anticipated the consequences.

———*ᴍᴍ*———

A few days before reaching Base Camp, a number of oxygen bottles were stolen from the Sodoc expedition. This could have had a crippling effect on the summit effort. Derek was furious and he and Reggie had a protracted argument over it. He also accused the Sherpa, given their history of theft. The result was a sharp decline in morale among them. The remaining bottles were moved from the side of the evening camp to the center and Reggie posted only the Sherpa he trusted to stand watch while everyone else slept.

Other disturbing events continued. The Italian team's ill health persisted. Benito Luci told me, "I've never experienced anything like that. First the runs, you know, having to go all the time. We were dehydrated and very tired from it. Then some of the climbers began to see things, delusions, you know? It was frightening. Somebody was doing something to us, I think."

———

The enormous Sodoc expedition stretched out some three miles like a giant languid snake by the time it reached Base Camp. It took half the day for the tail to reach the head. At 18,000 feet in elevation, Base Camp sits just below the notorious Ice Fall on a sloped patch of barren rock. At the height of the climbing season, twice each year, the camp has more than four hundred tents and is the largest village in this part of Nepal. It is an anthill of activity with its brightly colored tents, trash piles, and prayer flags.

The Sodoc expedition paraded through the camp until it reached the coveted site closest to the Everest passage. Since this had been set aside for them earlier, there existed a considerable measure of ill will toward Derek from those who were not part of the media circus. It is said that rank has its privileges, but it would be more accurate to say that the privileges come with wealth.

More than a dozen major expeditions were already scattered about Base Camp—three times the number of smaller outfits. These were fit—generally young—people, away from home and families. For many of the climbers—women as well as men—this was a time to party; the immediacy of danger and the possibility of death served as the ultimate aphrodisiac. The Sodoc expedition was no different in that regard.

It might be the size of a small town, but there is no legal authority at Base Camp. There is no zoning authority and there are no rules. Climbers erect their sites wherever they want. There are no logical pathways through the maze of tents, no system at all in this impromptu town. Though latrines and potties are set up beside the living area, climbers are known to relieve themselves between the tents at will. If the need strikes at night, no one moves more than a few feet from their tent to defecate. The consequence is an unpleasant odor that hangs over the tents, like that in a third world slum. And because sanitation is so casual and the local bacteria so exotic, intestinal illnesses are common, all but universal. With so many expeditions already in place, conditions were already in rapid decline.

Understandably, those first days at Base Camp were a media frenzy. A half-dozen camera crews from various television outlets were already in place. No matter their primary reason for being there, once Derek Sodoc arrived, he became part of the story. Cameramen scrambled for shots, maneuvering to keep one another out of the field of sight when recording. Derek and Tarja were the hottest couple on the planet. They beamed at the cameras, kissed like the newlyweds they were, and grinned.

SNS wanted the additional publicity and, to a certain extent, Derek cooperated with the other crews. Everywhere he went, he was filmed, though he gave no interviews to the others, reserving those for his own network. Everyone wanted his or her picture taken with the great explorer and he was generally agreeable, typically posing for more than an hour each day.

There were a fair number of young, fit women at the camp and Tarja couldn't help noticing. Mountain climbing—in particular, climbing the highest mountain on earth—appeals to a significant number of women. They are drawn to the adventure—or to the adventurers. As a result, Tarja stayed very close to her new husband, as if tethered to his side, a continuation of her role on the trek and one that was both new and humiliating for her.

"They threw themselves at him," a pal confides. "It was like that everywhere he went. They'd drop by the campsite at night and flaunt their wares. Tarja knew, of course. She'd done enough of the same herself to know what was what.

She did everything but run them off with a stick—especially Sabrina and that Jap girl."

The schedule in those first days was hectic. Crystal and Rusty were busy filming segments for SNS. The better the pieces, the more the network demanded. Ratings rose steadily from the first day the expedition arrived at Base Camp. The demand for them was all but insatiable.

It was a complicated process to produce these segments, all this filming, editing and uploading. The producers of Derek's popular television program, *High Adventure!* had provided Crystal with a list of topics for future use and she guided Derek through conversations structured to be used later. This made for a busy schedule unrelated to the serious business of actually climbing the mountain.

Derek's continued drug use only added to the difficulties. When Tarja used up her supply, she bought more at Base Camp, content to turn her husband into a zombie if necessary. Or so those there say. Many in the know add that the seeds of destruction were planted before anyone on the expedition so much as set a foot above Base Camp—though no one saw it at the time. If Derek's drug use was known, no one spoke of it. They ate, slept, and screwed in blissful, self-satisfied ignorance.

It's generally taken as a blessing when it snows at Base Camp, as a fresh blanket of clean snow covers the odors and contaminants that build up. For a time, the unpleasant odors are gone.

Sometimes the wind blows and it snows at the same time. It's not all that different from the Midwest. At the summit, the wind howls and the snow screams through the air. Sometimes, when it's clear at Base Camp, you can see the dark storm above, coiled about the summit like a death mask.

An irony of the great mountain is that the most dangerous portion of the climb is the Ice Flow immediately above Base

Camp. It is an ever-changing, deadly river of ice. Its sheer white canyons spike terror into the heart of even the most intrepid climber. There is no other way up the mountain from this side, so passage must regularly be made through it. A climber can do nothing in the Ice Fall that will make him or her safe. Climbers must rely on snow bridges that can give away without warning.

As for the primary purpose of the expedition, or what should have been its primary purpose, the path through the treacherous Ice Flow had already been carved and was being maintained by an expedition from Korea. They charged every climber each time he or she used it, making it the highest toll road in the world. There was, after all, only one best route each season. Other teams could create their own if they wanted, but it would take time and certainly cost lives. In the end, it would be an inferior, riskier path through a section of the mountain the teams and their Sherpa must pass many times.

Once the expedition was in place, Reggie and the Sherpa were busy moving supplies above the Ice Flow to the various staging camps. This is the first essential step after reaching Base Camp where supplies were relatively abundant—which would not be the case higher up. Tarja, to name just one, even possessed a number of luxuries others did not. For example, she never lacked for a fresh change of clothing. Her makeup and hair were prepared and styled each day by a plain, middle-aged woman from France named Marie. Though most of the food supplies were at the large dining tent, Tarja insisted that certain delicacies be kept close at hand. These reportedly included clams and truffles.

Above Base Camp, little is ferried that is not essential and such luxury is unknown. From here on, the Sherpa serve as beasts of burden and typically carry at least fifty pounds on each trip, returning the same day to spend the night below before repeating the process. They can descend very rapidly without the weight of a load.

As the supplies are moved up, a string of camps is set in place. At 19,500 feet, just above the Ice Flow, was Camp One. There were more than a dozen tents here and the larger expeditions each maintained one or two Sherpa to see to the needs of climbers moving up the mountain. As at Base Camp, meals were prepared and every morning climbers were roused by a hot mug of sweet tea.

Each of the high camps was located a four- to six-hour climb apart. All supplies were meticulously counted. Any unnecessary provisions carried higher was dangerous and a waste of needed man power. Too much risk and energy was required for every pound taken up.

A half-day's climb higher was Camp Two, at the Western Cwm. Situated at just over 21,000 feet, it was also called Advanced Base Camp because it was here that the expedition leaders such as Reggie typically called the shots. Except for cameramen, the media went no higher either. In fact, most crews had a relay station here, since sending signals down the mountain was always uncertain and the more places that could handle it, the more likely a signal could reach Base Camp. It was there that the actual editing and uploading took place.

ABC was the last place on the mountain with all the comforts of home. Sherpa still prepared the meals and saw to all the chores. From here on, each climber—with certain notable exceptions—was expected to prepare his or her own meals and see to every need.

Four hours higher up, at 24,400 feet, was Camp Three. Windy and cold, it was no place to linger and no one did willingly. Camp Four was at 26,000 feet, the beginning of the Death Zone. It was a miserable place, exposed to the wind, and tents were perched on a narrow blade of ice. From here on, the body underwent a slow death—even with oxygen—as the human body is simply not adapted to surviving at such an extreme altitude.

Next was a bivouac known as Camp Five. Unpleasant as was Camp Four, this was even worse. Cold and windy, climbers lay in a tent for a few hours before setting out for the summit. If they lay down there on the descent, more often than not, they died.

In addition to clearing and maintaining the passage through the Ice Flow, the Korean team also stretched a line through it. To this lifesaving line, each climber attached him or herself. Without it, the incidence of death on Everest would be ten times higher.

The line was fixed from the bottom of the Ice Flow all the way to the summit, in part by the Koreans as in the flow, in part by other teams, and finally by the first team to actually summit. Every team moving up maintains the line, so no fee is charged above the Ice Flow. The unspoken reality of Everest is that every climber—from the most skilled Sherpa to the least athletic amateur—is fastened to a secure line from Base Camp to the top of the world.

Though the passageway through the Ice Flow had been cleared, it still took three weeks to set up the camps and ferry supplies up in preparation for the summit assault. Twenty-one days is a long time, an eternity in certain conditions. So it was then.

The process of acclimatizing is amazing as well as essential. You cannot prepare to be very high on the mountain until you are there. Once the first of the higher camps was in place, Reggie instructed the climbers to hike up to Camp One for a few hours, then return to Base Camp. This had the effect of jumpstarting the build-up of corpuscles to carry vital oxygen. Even a relatively short time at a higher altitude kicked the body into high gear, as it had no way of knowing when you'd return—and from Mother Nature's perspective, it's better to be safe than sorry. It could always slough off the extra corpuscles if they weren't used.

This was followed some days later by a sleepover at Camp One, then a few hours at ABC the next morning, before returning to Base Camp. The process was exhausting—even for those in excellent shape. The body places great demands on itself as it produces the extra cells. There is no way to rush the process and that accounts in large part for why it took so long to set up the five camps. There is no point in rushing as the human body prepares itself for the summit assault.

In Base Camp, climbers undergoing the process lounged throughout the days and, once the process began in earnest, rutted at night—hard as that might be to believe. This was a result of the build-up of oxygen. As their blood count rose, the air at Base Camp became relatively richer and richer. It became a heady mix that season. Those acclimatizing felt better and better, and when you mix young men and women so far from home along with that sense of well-being and eternal life, the inevitable happens.

Though the temperature fell significantly after dark, Base Camp turned into a party. Sources there say that strong drink was widespread and that familiar pungent odor of strong ganja bought in Kathmandu drifted in the air. Stereos blared the latest pop, hip-hop, or Euro tech songs. The young and horny moved from camp to camp in search of excitement and a fresh companion for the night. Few were disappointed.

It was little different for the Sherpa—even though they were doing all the real work. The available women were busy indeed, spending time beneath more than one man every day. One of the young Sherpa men, who it was said was especially ugly and smelled, was even found seeking his comfort from an unprotesting yak.

At the foot of Everest, it was as if all rules were extinguished; nothing mattered so much as getting what you wanted and keeping the party going. It was a dangerous mix of frivolity and lust.

At night, Derek wandered among the tents, joined by Tarja, visiting and partying with the best or he remained sequestered in his own tent, freebasing with his young wife.

Oddly, or perhaps not so oddly, Crystal's anger at being spurned quickly turned away from Derek and planted itself firmly with Tarja. Tarja had stolen her man—that's what sources report Crystal said. It was obvious even before the expedition left for the hinterland that no love was lost between Crystal and Tarja. The bride found difficulty getting airtime and Crystal ignored her otherwise. Though pals say Crystal still pined for Derek, she kept her feelings close. She was, however, rarely alone at night. Perhaps seeing Derek with his new bride was more than she could take.

---

Not surprisingly, no interview with Derek ever appeared on Japanese television. "Tarja was a maniac and she had him under her thumb, the *ama* b\*\*\*h," Reiki says. "A shame. He was such a man. No one on that expedition let me near him after the trouble. Then we had to turn back."

It happened this way. At Base Camp, Tarja made it clear that she'd create a scene and make Derek wish he'd never been born if something wasn't done about "that yellow slant-eyed whore!" Derek and Reggie conferred and the next morning Reggie went to the Japanese crew and delivered the ultimatum. They had to return to Kathmandu.

"Can you believe it?" Reiki says. "For that, too. I told my crew we were staying. She'd get over it. Base Camp was busy and she'd have other things on her mind. They drugged Fuyuto or something after the knife incident. I don't know for sure, but he was in his tent all the time. Then we got a call from Tokyo that SNS had contacted them and said that if we didn't go back, SNS would break all ties with us. So I had no choice. When I got to Tokyo, they fired me. Now I'm working in a noodle shop. Is that fair?"

Some months later, Reiki appeared as the centerfold in the Japanese edition of *Playboy* magazine. There reportedly was a film contract—of what sort, you can imagine—so she didn't serve noodles for long (at least, not the skinny, limp kind).

This particular incident was a turning point of sorts. Whatever transpired between Derek and his wife in private remained. The hurt—the tension—simmered like a vile brew. For a time, Derek behaved himself and Tarja pretended that they were once again the happily married couple. It was, given the forces at work, nothing more than the lull before the deadly storm.

---

The situation deteriorated for the Italian crew at Base Camp. Upon her return, Sabrina told a Rome news agency, "I became very ill. I agree with Benito that someone was messing with our food supply. There was a dirty little Sherpa hanging around our cook at the time. We couldn't get rid of him. I was too sick to go on."

Benito agrees. "It wasn't just us, either. Once we reached Base Camp, other teams became ill as well. The bigger expeditions had no trouble; they guarded their water and food, but several smaller teams went back when we did. It's dirty to play like that. I don't know who did it to us, but I have a pretty good idea."

---

Three days into the portage to the higher camps, disaster struck. Gyurme, the lovable and competent Sherpa leader, was caught beneath a wall of ice that fell on him in the Ice

Flow. It was fortunate that he was the only one to die. Such incidents often take four or five Sherpa at a time.

It was not possible to recover his body and it lies up there still. The next day, the Sherpa gathered at the ever-growing rock prayer mound beside Base Camp to string fresh flags for their fallen leader and to pray. The names of some of the greatest climbers in history, both Westerners and Sherpa, are inscribed on those rocks. The mound grows every climbing season with the addition of more stones and prayer flags. No greater single monument to courage exists in the entire world.

The Sherpa respectfully raised the fallen tattered flags tied to lines and set them in place. They built an altar on the mound where they laid sprigs of juniper incense, which they lit. They placed about bits of food, beer, and tea. It was meant to appeal to the gods and they were never certain what the gods would want. This done, they raised bright new flags—one containing Gyurme's name—knelt on prayer rugs, and were led in chants.

This is the Puja ceremony. Sherpa believe that the gods are everywhere—in the forest, the soil, even the very air we breathe. They must pay attention to them and give homage. They also believe that ghosts are all about and it is best to avoid them if at all possible, since they wish man only evil. They have for this reason an aversion for the dead.

They took the opportunity of the Puja to invoke blessings on the pending climb. Placed at the mound were crampons, ice axes, and harnesses, to be blessed. The Sherpa believe that the gods decide who lives and who dies—every one of them sought personal favor so he could avoid the fate of their leader.

The death, those on the climb report, had a sobering effect on the Sherpa, even though death is the common currency on Everest. Sherpa guides die like mayflies every year on the mountain; as Buddhists, they're resigned to their fate. Believing in karma, their religion teaches that they will return to live again. They believe they pay in this life for what they've done in their previous one. In other words, they believe that there are no free passes. That was something the Westerners had yet to learn.

Religion, or what others might call superstition, plays a vital role in the life of the Sherpa in any number of ways. For example, every few years in Nepal, a living goddess, known as the Kumari, is selected from a group of four-year-olds. This follows an elaborate, months-long selection process. The Kumari is believed to be the physical incarnation of a goddess until her first menstrual cycle, when it is thought that the goddess flees her body. Then a replacement is selected.

For the years of her existence, the Kumari lives a life of absolute privilege, cared for by servants in a palace. It is thought she can see the future though she gives no sign of it. She does not speak or move during her brief audiences. Instead, her attendant interprets her facial expressions and reactions.

Several of these living goddesses are selected in various parts of Nepal. The Sherpa had been honored earlier when one of their own was chosen. It was a source of immense pride to the people. Then, just months before the Sodoc expedition, the Kumari had been demoted and declared no longer a living goddess, a great shame to the people. There were those on the expedition who expected bad things to happen because if it. They turned out to be prophetic.

Tsongba, small and quiet, a cousin of the fallen leader, took over as head Sherpa. As it turned out, Gyurme was only a warning of what was to come. Perhaps the Sherpa are right and man's destiny is decided by the mother goddess, Sagarmatha.

~~~

Interestingly, the leader of the Nepalese expedition had been an escort for the Kumari the previous summer. Girija Dahal had gone to Bangkok where she gave her interview. Her departure from the kingdom of Nepal led to her defrocking and he was quite outspoken about what took place on that weeklong trip.

In an interview with the BBC Worldwide Service, he said, "There is no question of impropriety involving the goddess herself. She was properly chaperoned the entire time. I saw to that personally, though there was no need. Those assigned directly to her care were most attentive. The problem was with the attendants. This rich American—this Mr. Derek Sodoc— took advantage of them. They were from the country and were simple village girls. He overwhelmed them. I observed him coming out of their rooms at the hotel very late at night and once early in the morning. It was dishonorable.

"It was wrong to defrock the goddess as she committed no error. Her trip received approval. I think the priests who did it heard the stories about her attendants and feared she would be tainted in the retelling. You know how people are, how quickly they are willing to assume the worse. Mr. Sodoc was directly responsible for what happened, and in that regard bears responsibility for many deaths, including his own. We stayed away from him. He was poison."

Others say members of the Nepalese expedition were not so tolerant. One Sherpa told me, "We were very angry when we learned this was the man who abused our goddess. There were climbers with us who thought he should die for what he did. I know one of the women became pregnant because of him and killed herself. The man deserved what happened. I will say no more."

—*mm*—

At this time, Calvin began drawing blood from the Westerners who would be higher up the mountain. He carefully monitored their cell count—even administering certain drugs as needed. Climbers would carry a supply of pills to be taken only if required. Derek was taking no chances.

Still, it should not be forgotten that even Base Camp sits at an elevation much higher than we are used to. Even there, bad things can happen. Two days after Gyurme's death, Tarja's stylist fell ill. She had not been well prepared for the expedition, being middle-aged and not especially fit. She'd struggled on the trek, but had gamely trudged on.

For several days, she'd looked unwell. Tarja was seen shouting at the woman over her inability to do her job. A few days later, she was found unconscious in her tent. "It was frightening," a source says. "We thought she was dead at first. Doc checked and found she was breathing, but just barely. She was suffering from high-altitude sickness. He gave her an injection and she revived a bit. That same day, she was placed on a litter and carried back down the mountain. I heard she recovered fully. Tarja refused to pay her and was enraged she had to do her own hair after that."

Marie gave *Paris Match* an interview. "She is evil, that woman. I almost died for her and she spits in my face. Who will pay my bills? I ask you. She should burn in hell for what she did to me."

The death and illness proved ill omens. Though the weather on the trek to Base Camp had been glorious, it deteriorated once the expedition was in place. The gentle days were replaced by dark, rolling clouds and stiff winds. As a consequence, the movement of supplies up the mountain was often hindered and the major expeditions already there were prevented from making their summit push. Light overnight snowstorms were common. These would be followed by two or three days of brilliant though deceptive weather. No benign weather pattern emerged of sufficient duration to permit an assault on the summit.

The Sherpa came to view the Westerners and their actions with disdain and disgust—even hatred. "None of us wanted to be on the mountain that year," one told me. "Our goddess had been defiled. It was a bad sign. The priests told us to stay home with our wives and children, to pray that year. When the expedition men came to hire for the climb, we refused at first. But they increased the money. We are poor. What could we do?"

The unease was apparent throughout the Sherpa guides— not just those on the Sodoc expedition, but with the others as well. Lacking was the usual enthusiasm to climb, the unfailing good nature of the men. Instead, they prayed more than usual and, when things did not go well, cast sullen— often angry and disgusted—looks at their own leaders and the Westerners.

"We thought about going back when Gyurme died in the Ice Flow. It was bad to lose your leader before you have even left Base Camp. Many of us wanted to. Then Tsongba was elected leader and he said we had to go up. There was much arguing about it. Then they gave us more money."

The Sherpa know why it all turned out so badly. "They were wicked people. They did not respect the gods. The mountain is not to be treated like that. She will get her revenge, always. That is what happened. We should not have gone."

When the bloom is off the rose, when the lovely days of hiking turn into cold, wet days of slogging, when the specter of death greets you at every turn, you know more is at stake than your reputation—the overriding question becomes: *Will I get down alive?*

It was a question every climber on the expedition would soon encounter. The primary problem was becoming apparent.

It was not the weather. It was not the death of the Sherpa or even a treacherous passage through the Ice Flow. The pervasive problem was that there was one way up the mountain. Time was the enemy of opportunity for this large amount of climbers—and more were arriving with each passing day. In other words, there would soon be a traffic jam on the mountain.

Derek was anxious to fulfill his destiny to complete his ring of seven. His goal was widely known, but not all members of the group cared, especially the Sherpa. All climbers at Base Camp knew they were going to reach the top as well and, though they were glad to have their photograph taken with the famous adventurer, no one would let Derek's attempt get in their way.

The problem was magnified because some of the climbers considered this their only chance to climb Mount Everest. If they failed this year, they would get no second chance. They were not disposed to be charitable. In addition, the climbers who had paid big money to the major expeditions, in excess of $100,000 in some cases, believed that they had been promised that they would summit. Every climber expected to get the photograph of themselves they actually wanted, not one of them with Derek Sodoc, but of them standing astride the peak.

Also, all the financial organizers of the other expeditions were under pressure to perform, and get their clients to the top. They planned to put everyone who paid for the opportunity on the summit, if at all possible. The consequence was that Derek didn't matter to them in reality; poster boy or not.

It was apparent early on that too many climbers were planning to use this route up the mountain. Mysterious and unexplained bouts of illness struck many of the teams. Upward of a dozen turned back as a result. The theft of equipment was epidemic at Base Camp and at least six teams were unable to attempt the summit. Still, a significant number of climbers remained.

In an attempt to coordinate the various efforts, Reggie called a meeting of the significant expedition leaders to work out a schedule and agree to rules of conduct. However, for the most part, what was entered into wasn't followed. The problem was the weather and other on-site issues nullified most, if not all their agreements. In such a place, at such a time, in the face of so many conflicting demands, no one's word meant anything. What ruled was a perverse form of jungle law—survival of the fittest.

There was no other law and no police. There was simply no way to compel anyone to do anything—especially since most would never see one another again. Every society works because of a certain level of coercion or social pressure. On Everest, neither of these existed.

"We didn't trust or like them," the leader of one small team told me in an exclusive interview. "We all thought they were the ones making trouble. I can't say Derek was in on it, maybe he just turned a blind eye, but they had a couple of nasty Sherpa on their team. Those guys showed up at the oddest times. All of us were forced to post guards in the end if we wanted to climb. Those who were careless had to turn back."

Even those associated with the Sodoc team hint that this team leader might well have it right. Sources reveal that there was a lot of late-night talk in Sodoc's tent about what to do with all the climbers. It wasn't long before amicable solutions were rejected.

"We tried that already. F**k them all," Derek finally announced. "I've been more than fair to these people. We've got the numbers and we've got the guides. We'll just take control of the route."

In the end, the expedition resorted to unscrupulous tactics at Base Camp. On the route up, they simply bullied their way to the top. There were complaints and a few media reports were filed about the expedition's aggression. But SNS controlled the media message; the image Crystal uploaded and the storyline that New York produced were the ones that dominated the airwaves.

The truth is not very nice, but that's the way it was.

—⁓⁓⁓—

Derek's cocaine use continued at Base Camp. Doc Cal was heard more than once arguing with him over it, telling him he was in no condition to climb. He even spoke to Tarja, the enabler, but to no avail. "It was like she didn't care what happened to him," a disgusted climber told me. "Considering what happened, that's as close to the truth as we'll ever get. Everything that followed was really inevitable."

—⁓⁓⁓—

Until this point, despite all the problems both known and unknown to the team members, matters had gone relatively well for the Sodoc expedition. At night, the party continued to the beat of a hundred radios. Climbers changed partners in their never-ending orgy. Reporters filed stories; everyone had their pictures taken with everyone else.

During the day, as they waited for summit weather and their bodies to create a suitable blood count, all faces turned to the great hulking mass rising ominously above. Despite brave words and assurances, they could not help but be intimidated. No one contemplating that climb can lie to themselves forever about the risk. Along the route above, lie the unavoidable dead—each a reminder of what can be and of the fate a portion of them are certain to suffer.

Beside Base Camp is the prayer mound, flags flapping in the wind, fading photographs scattered among the gray rock, and the names etched in stone. The Sherpa paid almost daily devotions there—especially those about to move up. The clanging of cymbals, burning of incense, the incantations could not be missed and neither could their implications.

For the Sherpa, there is no doubt. The mountain goddess decides who lives and who dies. Like the rest of the alternatives in their short existence, the logic is simple. For the Westerners, it was more complicated and much less reassuring.

―――――

Derek's sexual misdeeds along the trail had not continued at Base Camp, in large part because of Tarja. Derek had no choice and behaved himself—whether he wanted to or not.

Sabrina came around a few times, but never made it beyond the perimeter of the Sodoc camp. "There was something I needed to tell him," she later wrote. "In the end, I suppose it wouldn't have been important to him." Unconfirmed reports are that she had had an abortion a few weeks later.

But life and fidelity are not that easy, nor are fundamental problems within a marriage so readily overcome. It all unraveled about two weeks after the expedition reached Base Camp.

The inclement weather had abated and the summit attempt was about to begin. Derek and Doc Calvin had been to Advanced Base Camp for a night as part of their acclimatization process. A brief period of benign weather prevailed and climbers in other expeditions had scurried up the route toward the top. Derek was eager to move up before the various campsites were overwhelmed with numbers, but was not yet physically ready. Regardless, the higher camps were not adequately stocked for the attempt.

Things were on track as the pair returned to Base Camp in high spirits. The climbing had gone well and, if the weather held, there was a good likelihood that Derek would be moving up within a few days. Euphoric over events, off drugs for several days, and in the relatively rich air of a lower elevation, Derek was feeling his oats.

For hundreds of years, slavers have traveled to Nepal from India to steal Nepalese girls to sell into prostitution. Indians consider them beautiful and sexually desirable. To see the Sherpa women on the trail and at the mountain carrying supplies—deeply tanned, a hard life in the sun emblazoned on their skin—it's hard to imagine. Still, there were exceptions.

After that night's dinner, once again high on cocaine, Derek excused himself to use one of the portable potties, but was gone a moment or two longer than Tarja thought reasonable. She stalked off in search of her errant husband and found him behind a boulder going at it with the youngest Sherpa woman. She caught Derek at the moment of orgasm.

"He was beyond caring in that instant," a source said. "The earth could have opened up and swallowed him and he'd not have noticed. Between the sex and the drugs, he had no idea where he was or what he was doing."

As Derek adjusted his trousers, he spotted his irate wife and immediately tried to make light of the incident, but Tarja would have none of that. She was furious, screaming, chasing the poor Sherpa woman, and striking her husband. Our international beauty had taken all she could stand. Derek's cheating had been consistent ever since the marriage, though the new Mrs. Sodoc was only now understanding that.

As Tarja walked about the camp that night, she could see the way others looked at her. Never in all her life had she been humiliated in such a way. Anger and shame were written across her face.

"It was great," a pal says, "watching her get her comeuppance. Nobody liked her. We were having a great time of it. And she knew it."

Defining as the event should have been, wives have tolerated worse—and Tarja was prepared to swallow her pride. That night, she reconciled with Derek. We can only imagine at what personal price to her. The pair retired early—and conspicuously—to their tent. For the next few days, as preparations to move up were advanced, the two were inseparable. It seemed that all was forgiven.

Then a very angry Tarja paid a hasty call on Doc Calvin. She'd contracted gonorrhea.

"We heard about it at once," a source says. "There are no secrets on Everest. It wasn't Doc. But we knew. And laughed like hell."

This was the last straw. It was one thing for her husband to sleep with an attractive Italian or an equally attractive Japanese reporter. It was bearable, just, for him to rut in the open with a disgusting Sherpa. But giving her a venereal disease he'd contracted from the woman was beyond the pale. Tarja was humiliated and very angry. He had demeaned her in everyone's eyes—and he was going to pay.

"Everything changed for her at that point. From the time she'd caught him with his trousers around his ankles, people looked at her differently. They'd joked behind her back, but now she was a laughingstock," a former pal told me.

Tarja slept alone that night. In fact, Derek had shared her tent and the pleasure of her body for the final time. He saw Doc Cal and, for a few days, neither of them was especially active. The weather delayed events as it was, so no extra time was lost.

Then Peer was seen ducking into Tarja's tent. "They weren't strangers," a source says. "Tarja and Peer knew one another from her time as an Olympic competitor. Though she never competed in the Olympics, she had participated in a number of international meets. It was then that she met Peer and the two of them went at it hot and heavy." Now the relationship was resumed and Derek was shut out.

As with captains of sailing ships, the Sherpa believe that a woman on the mountain is bad luck. How they explain their own women there is a mystery, though they allow none above Base Camp. But Tarja was not content merely to have an affair. No, this was about much more. It was about punishing Derek. It was about making him suffer as she had suffered.

Until this moment, Derek had never been the one to pay. He was the one who ended relationships. If anyone paid a price, it was always the woman. All that changed now. If Tarja had not liked the way the other climbers looked at her after these events, clearly Derek did not like how he was seen once his wife took up with Peer. But his account was long overdue and his wife was now going to see that it was paid in full.

It is the nature of such climbs that climbers develop a shared congeniality. Respect is the rule for those who seek the greatest prize of mountaineering. When friendship turns to suspicion, trouble is inevitable.

Derek resumed his relationship with Crystal that night and they remained lovers until the day of his tragic death high atop the world.

～⁓⁓⁓～

The Sherpa say the mountain goddess passes judgment. And so it seemed from that day forward. The Sherpa notice everything. They are attuned to the mountain in ways Westerners can never be. The mountain is the heart and soul of their religion. They were increasingly uneasy over events, going so far as to resist going up the mountain. There was an unprecedented work stoppage and Reggie was forced to increase wages to get the movement of supplies resumed. The Sherpa spent more time in prayer and even greater hours talking in hushed voices among themselves.

The good days were now permanently behind the expedition. From this point on, the Sodoc expedition experienced equipment failures, increasing bouts of illness, and scheduling conflicts with New York.

Doc finally had his way and Derek knocked off the drugs. Perhaps it was because he no longer had access to his source. Perhaps he was thinking more clearly. Regardless, he detoxed, though once the worst of that was over, he wasn't his customary self. His good nature eroded. He became short-tempered, difficult to talk to, and even more difficult to influence in a positive way.

Tarja, invigorated by her decision, strutted about Base Camp as if she hadn't a care in the world. When Peer went up the mountain for two days, she spent the night in the tent of a female Polish climber. She even mentioned it over lunch to be certain that there was no doubt about what she'd been doing.

On camera, Derek's engaging manner now failed him utterly. Concerns were expressed and he received a call from his father telling him that the quality of programming was now substandard. The rebuke clearly stung.

We can be certain that this had never happened before. In all his life, for all his riches and toys, with his privileged existence, never had a woman made him pay the way that Tarja did in those final days of his life.

Perhaps, some say, she had him pay the ultimate price as well.

# Modern Gear Makes Climbing Better, But Not Easier, or Safer

Climb Everest website
Posted May 29

High-tech gear dominates Everest climbing expeditions. The latest example of this climbing axiom is the Sodoc Foundation Everest expedition, now nearing the crucial summit attempt window. But when adventurer Derek Sodoc steps on the summit of Mt. Everest, he will have advantages that few climbers in history have enjoyed.

Satellite telephones will have kept him—and those climbing with him—in near-constant contact with Base Camp. He can even call home if he wants. Those assisting have rugged laptops with which they track the latest weather patterns, always key as weather kills far more often than do falls or illness.

The expedition has its own doctor, a specialist in high-altitude climbing, as well as a plethora of modern drugs that make acclimatization easier and quicker than ever before.

In addition, contemporary climbing gear is lighter and more rugged than any employed previously. Most importantly, oxygen tanks, which will be used on the final push, are lighter and contain more oxygen than ever before.

But for all of his advantages, Sodoc will still have to climb the mountain by himself. He will not be carried to the top—nor will he transported there. He will conquer it one step at a time, as all have before him.

And stalking him up the flank of that enormous edifice will be the same specter of death that has haunted every would-be conqueror of the highest point on earth. Despite all the advantages modern climbers enjoy, the death toll mounts with every year. We wish Derek the very best of luck.

# Chapter Five

# An Angry Goddess

The brief window of summit weather turned erratic again. Other expeditions with their own schedules and concerns, or perhaps wanting to escape what was clearly the Sodoc expedition's bad karma, set out for the summit now in bursts, depending on opportunity. They moved from high camp to higher camp as the weather dictated, clogging the choke points, and making it difficult for the Sodoc expedition to properly plan its own assault on the peak. When the two next biggest expeditions set out, the Sodoc team was crestfallen.

"I can't say we sabotaged any of the other teams. I know those accusations have been made. True, there were thefts of oxygen bottles, but we had some stolen from us. Someone was up to something, but it wasn't us. As far as I knew, the plan was to manage the other expeditions," a source confided. "No one had ever seen anything like it, certainly not on Everest. But still … there is only so much that can be done. Climbers at crucial points cannot be bodily moved aside. It just isn't done. Those other expeditions and lines of climbers were potentially a serious problem for Derek, who was under enormous pressure to produce."

This was a problem not appreciated in Manhattan. The men in suits were accustomed to telling reporters in the field to get the story and deliver the product on schedule—no matter what. They did not know—or perhaps did not care—about the special difficulties an Everest expedition encounters. Derek's strain and worry were obvious and he became increasingly short-tempered and erratic in his decisions.

Reggie was also under increasing pressure to get Derek to the top. There had been some foolish talk about the Sodoc expedition being the first to summit that year. This was not realistic—especially since so many climbers had left while the expedition was still in Kathmandu. From the flurry of reports and special coverage, you'd have thought no one had ever climbed Everest before.

"SNS international headquarters was devastated when the first team summited and it wasn't theirs. They'd managed to convince themselves that Derek would be the first on top that year. That's how out of touch they were," a source says. "There were nasty sat phone conversations with Derek and Reggie about it, I can tell you. Marketing had its plans and Derek was being pressured to conform."

When the other climbers began to summit, the natural consequence was that some of the steam was released from the storyline. They'd been covering it hard for weeks and it wasn't possible to sustain that level. New York demanded a summit climb before public interest waned entirely. Ratings were very important.

Derek was told to get to the top ASAP—preferably during East Coast prime time. The sheer logistics of such an effort were daunting. The weather and the existence of so many other climbers made the task even more difficult.

But before the Sodoc expedition was ready to set out, two of the major expeditions had summited. The positive consequence was that some of the traffic on the route up eased.

Another advantage of their going first was that they had also cleared the way to the top, fixing line from the Ice Flow to the summit. This meant that the following expeditions could reach the top in a much shorter period of time than the early ones had.

The storyline had been for Derek and his bride to summit together. Certainly that had been the publicity to this point and expectations were high. Plus, Tarja had insisted from day one. But now, with so much water under the bridge, the two were estranged and, on Everest at least, it was clear that the lovebirds weren't climbing the mountain together. While Derek sought solace in the arms of his producer, orgasmic cries from his wife's tent during visits from Peer could be heard by anyone within earshot. Only a porn star with the name Sally the Screamer had louder sex.

"Derek's embarrassment was acute," a pal said. "You couldn't help but feel sorry for the man. Here he was coming off a serious drug binge and there was Tarja putting on quite a show. To be frank, though, we all wanted some of that."

As push-off day approached, Reggie orchestrated a meeting between Derek and Tarja in an attempt to bring the rancor to an end. Doc was there to keep order. The meeting was grim, according to a little bird that was there and told me all.

"I don't know what's happened between you two," Reggie began. "But we need to get this worked out."

Tarja shot Derek an unpleasant look. "If he can manage to keep it buttoned for a few days, I'm willing to do my part." It was only natural; Tarja had the most to lose if this didn't happen.

Derek had been morose, staring toward the back of the tent. "Why don't you put a sock in it when you screw, okay? The whole camp can hear you."

"Jealous? Peer's a stud. He was always the best."

"Knock it off, you two!" Reggie said. "This is no place for such childishness. A climber died up there yesterday. Had you heard? This is dangerous business. Either you work together—or, Tarja, you're off the attempt."

She glared at Reggie. "If I get dropped, I'll turn this publicity stunt into a charade. Do you hear me, hubby dear? I'm climbing. That's all there is to it."

Derek refused to give in—until Reggie finally suggested a solution. "Derek, you and Tarja pretend to make up, all right? This is business and it's in both your interests to climb the bloody thing. No one off the mountain knows what's going on and, if someone posts something, surely SNS can bury the story."

"I'm not climbing with Peer—and that's final!" Derek shouted.

"He has to summit. You know that," Reggie said. "I've specific instructions from New York."

Derek was soon on the satellite phone with New York, but Peer was important to the company's plans to market in Europe. SNS was engaged in a significant European expansion and Peer was an important part of that. Derek disconnected without comment.

It was agreed that Tarja would stop seeing Peer and, in exchange, she would still summit with her husband. Everyone would pretend that nothing had happened. Since SNS essentially controlled the storyline on the mountain, they believed they could get away with it.

Tarja was clearly interested in pursuing her independent career. Summiting was as important to her as it was to Derek, so she agreed. Plus, she'd already made her point. However, there remained a fly in the ointment—a Norwegian fly.

In the end, a compromise was reached at Doc's suggestion. The summit team was divided in two. Derek and his wife were on Team One; Peer and Scott Devlon comprised Team Two, which would depart just ten minutes later. The teams would be presented to the world as a single unit, when in fact they would be distinct. Very reluctantly, Derek agreed—with the understanding that he would never have to deal with Peer.

The final night in Base Camp was awkward. Derek and Tarja were still not talking to one another. Crystal was behaving as if nothing out of the ordinary was up. The Sherpa held a special service at the mound. Tsongba, their new leader, had to meet with them again to convince some of those still reluctant to simply do the job they'd been paid for.

And so, with great fanfare, the happy couple set out to conquer the highest point on earth. Derek was now going to play his own version of King of the Mountain. With the latest technology, long-range weather forecasts, the most experienced guides, and surrounded by stalwart friends, how could he fail?

But the Sherpa, only marginally persuaded by Tsongba, looked on with stoic faces and a solemn manner. Things were going badly because Derek was being punished for having sex with the Sherpa woman. It was one thing for her to have sex with them, but it was quite another to bend over for a Westerner. Her behavior had shamed not only her husband and her clan, but the expedition as well.

There was also the matter of the defrocked goddess. There were those among the Sherpa who now accepted that they were being punished for that great dishonor. The shaman had warned them not to climb and they'd allowed themselves to be persuaded with double wages. More than one now believed that they'd done the wrong thing.

"I wouldn't have wanted to climb with any of them. They're good men, but they were very unhappy," a source said. "When you are dealing with superstitious natives, it's always best to stay the hell away. They were clearly agitated. I know both Reggie and that Tsongba laid into that bunch to get them moving up the mountain."

Ahead of the Sodoc expedition was the Nepalese team, including those most adamant in their anger toward Derek.

Girija was quoted in a magazine saying, "My guides and climbers did not like the idea that we would be clearing the way for Mr. Sodoc. I told them we cleared the path for ourselves and should not concern ourselves with who followed. We were very sick as it was. I wasn't certain we could even make it to the top."

Asked about reports that a trailing Sherpa loosened ropes and supports, he denied them. "No one wanted to see anyone die—not by our hand at least. Death was up to the mountain and it needed no help from us—no matter how well deserved."

The two Sodoc teams climbed to Advanced Base Camp that first day. The departure was covered live by SNS during a special half-hour report following the evening news. The great theater was watched by millions around the globe. Tarja was her beaming best, waving gaily at those remaining in camp who clapped as they set out, then granting a misty, come-hither smile to the camera lens. Derek, resplendent in his orange high-altitude climbing suit, played his role, smiling warmly, waving jauntily, and placing his arm across her shoulders to pose for the cameras.

Everyone on the expedition knew what was really going on, but the world only knew what the network allowed them to see.

As well as everything had gone until now, even with the more frequent problems and intermittent benign weather, events now began to go very wrong—and you didn't have to be a Sherpa to see it. The climbers couldn't help but feel that more terrible things were yet to happen and bad things on Everest invariably meant death.

Two of the major expeditions had already summited and departed. Three others were planning to make their attempt at the same time. Money was discreetly handed out to some of the lesser expeditions to persuade them to delay their climb and at least one of the remaining large expeditions is reported to have been secretly paid to wait until after Derek's summit attempt.

But the Nepalese team moved up and so did one from Austria, as did some of the smaller expeditions who'd refused payment. The inevitable result was that the chokepoints up the mountain became crowded once again.

Team One consisted of Reggie, Rusty Landon who was filming Derek and Tarja, Tsongba and two experienced climbing Sherpa, one of whom carried equipment for Rusty. Crystal remained at Advanced Base Camp to download Rusty's feeds and to provide uplinks to New York. It was hoped, indeed was expected, that there would be an abundance of live shots from Everest.

All the climbers were given radios so that they could speak one to another as well as down to Advanced Base Camp. All the filming was done by Rusty. "It was actually a lean operation made possible by digital technology. Tarja objected, wanting at least two cameras so she'd get plenty of face time, but Derek stuck with Rusty," a knowledgeable source says.

That first night at Advanced Base Camp, Reggie took Scott aside and told him his responsibilities. "You're here to help your friend Derek summit," he said. "If all goes well, continue with him to the top. What matters first is his safety. After that, extend any assistance you can. I know I can rely on you because you're his friend. I know he is depending on you. We need someone to go with Peer so it isn't apparent what is really going on." Reggie looked at Scott intently. "Derek's distracted right now and under enormous pressure. I don't trust his judgment. I'm counting on you."

Scott nodded solemnly. "You can count on me," he said. Why he later forgot his promise, he's never explained.

That night at Advanced Base Camp, Derek and Tarja had an ugly argument. It began in their tent, which they'd agreed to share. Their voices became louder and louder until every-one could hear them through the nylon and over the wind. Finally Tarja stormed out of the tent, followed a moment later by a red-faced Derek.

The climbers were not yet on oxygen, so all the fighting left the pair coughing and hacking, but it was soon clear that there would be no mutual summit for the briefly happily-married couple. Reggie met with Scott and Peer and told them that Tarja would be returning to Base Camp the next morning.

It should be understood that none of the other Western climbers cared about any of this. By this time, they were all consumed with summit fever themselves. Like an epidemic, it had swept over the expedition. It is a difficult phenomenon to adequately describe. It is called a "fever" because those taken with it behave much as does a man finding himself in the grip of hot fever. Every thought—every moment—is taken up with a preoccupation of what has consumed him.

The infected climbers talked among themselves of noth-ing but getting to the top of the world. Every climber wanted nothing so much as to summit Everest. The fever consumed them all. All the long days from Kathmandu to the foothills of Nepal, up the side of the enormous mountain, was meant for this time. They all paid lip service to the idea of helping Derek, but in their hearts they all wanted the same thing—to climb that damn mountain.

---

By this time, all the climbers suffered the effects of altitude—even with the acclimatization they'd undergone. No one feels well on Everest, not even the Sherpa. There was not a Westerner on the expedition who'd not experienced a bout of diarrhea along the trek or at Base Camp. At high altitude, everyone suffers from headaches. It's like a sixteen-penny nail being driven through your head. And everyone coughs.

You cough until you think your lungs are going to come out. Some coughed until they spit up blood. Others, like Derek, coughed until they broke a rib.

That night at Advanced Base Camp was clear and cold. An incessant wind beat against the tent with a constant drubbing sound that made it difficult to rest and sleep. No one was consuming oxygen from the valuable containers that had been moved up, so everyone experienced a sensation of suffocation. Climbers awakened from shallow sleep certain they were going to die. The chronic shortness of breath also created a pervasive anxiety that permeated every decision a climber made. To climb Everest is to experience a sort of misery unknown anywhere else.

The next morning, the sun rose to a bright, clear, bitterly cold day. At very high altitude, climbers resemble the Pillsbury doughboy in their jumpsuits. They waddle about awkwardly, unable to move freely, as much a prisoner of their attire as anything else. In any other place, it would be amusing. Here it was just one more reminder of their bizarre existence.

"You need to go back down," Calvin reportedly told Derek. "You're not in shape for the big push. I think one of your ribs is cracked. You need to return to Base Camp to recuperate."

Derek was hearing none of that. "That's not possible. It has to be now. We have a window and I must take advantage of it."

"Listen to me, Derek. I mean it. You can't climb because the weather allows it or New York has given you a deadline or your father wants it. This is your life I'm talking about. You can't always be lucky. You're in no condition to climb. I just spent the night in the tent with you. I know."

Derek grinned. "Not to worry. I'm in the best of hands."

A few minutes later, a resigned Doc Cal administered a round of drugs. All the climbers had been on baby aspirin since arriving at Base Camp. Once they moved up, Doc had given them Diamox. This forced the kidneys to excrete bicarbonate that re-acidified the blood. The effect was to balance the effects of hyperventilation and to act as a respiratory stimulant, especially at night. But the effects were not predictable or consistent and the higher the climbers went, the less effective the drug would be.

Every climber was now given a supply of Decadron as well. This was a potent steroid used to treat brain swelling. It was, however, significantly different from Diamox. Whereas Diamox treated the problems associated with acclimatization, Decadron treated the symptoms caused by hypoxia, like taking a pill for pain while doing nothing about the underlying cause. It effectively removes the symptoms of AMS for a few hours and, for that reason, was invaluable. It is carried only to be used in an emergency. Calvin provided an extra supply to Derek with a cautionary word not to use it excessively.

When Reggie called a team meeting, the climbers stood about with their backs to the wind like cattle in the storm. The intrepid Rusty hoisted a shoulder camera and busied himself recording preparations.

Derek was distracted and clearly unhappy. Peer was distant, even sullen. Tarja remained angry and hostile. And Scott, Derek's good friend, was excited. The summit bug had bitten him well and deep. It was, essentially, going to be "to hell with Derek."

The plan called for Calvin to remain at Advanced Base Camp to await the return of the two teams from the summit. He would then move up to Camp Four to meet them and provide such medical care as was required.

This was a wise decision and typical of the care he gave. It was distressingly common for climbers descending the mountain to be in need of medical help. Climbers often exhausted themselves attaining the summit and found themselves without reserves of strength or the stamina to get back down. Frostbite was common and climbers were susceptible to injuries of every kind.

In their childlike state above Camp Four, judgment became impaired. More deaths occur on the descent than occur on the climb. Climbers wander off cliffs and fall to their deaths. Climbers find themselves unable to negotiate Hillary Step and die on the line. But most of all, climbers become exhausted. Moving is hard, stopping is easy. They sit down to rest just a few moments and then later lie down to sleep—a sleep from which they never awaken.

Frostbite, HACE, dementia, and exhaustion were the Four Horsemen of every summit attempt. Calvin intended to be in position to save lives at Camp Four.

That morning the Sherpa distributed breakfast tea to everyone. Once outside their tent, each climber buttoned up their high-altitude jumpsuits and rigged their gear. Derek was the only climber with an orange suit. New York had insisted on this so that viewers would always know him from the other climbers. Reggie wore a blue jumpsuit and about his neck was a red scarf knitted by his wife in New Zealand and given to him the previous Christmas. Tarja, naturally, was dressed in crimson.

At Advanced Base Camp, Crystal and Tarja exchanged ugly words and called each other vulgar names. Absurd as it seems in retrospect, Tarja took this moment to vent about Crystal's affair with her husband while Crystal accused Tarja of doing Peer. It was nasty and utterly out of place. Derek tried to put a stop to it, but realized soon enough that the pair wouldn't listen to him. Reggie stood aside and simply grimaced while the others stayed out of it as well.

"You had to see it to believe it. Here everyone was about to climb Everest and these two bitches were at it," a pal said. "But they soon ran out of steam since neither of them could breathe after a few minutes. They just stood there glaring at each other, sucking deep breaths."

Returning to work, Crystal attempted to interview Derek before their departure.

"Derek," she said, "let's get a shot with the mountain behind you. Come on."

"How many times do we have to do that one?" he complained. "If I'm sick of standing still for it, the viewers must be really sick of seeing it."

"It's the killer shot, trust me."

Rusty maneuvered the camera and then signaled that he was ready. "How do you feel as you set out, Derek?" Crystal asked.

"How the hell do you think I feel? Like shit!"

"Derek, we're recording. I'm not making conversation here. Try the answer again, please."

Derek drew several deep breaths and said, "I'm excited." He glanced toward the mountain behind him. "You can't help... Ah shit. What am I saying?"

And so it went. His concentration lagged and he stammered repeatedly. They were at it for ten minutes, but never got the shot she was after. Finally, Crystal terminated the interview. Derek was simply distracted on a day when he needed every ounce of his concentration to be on the task ahead of him. His marital and other problems were clearly taking a toll on his normally confident disposition.

Some thought they detected fear as he set off, but that could not have been the case. Here was a man who had faced death a thousand times before, a man who went out of his way to embrace danger. No, if he knew fear that was later—much later—when the possibility of his ultimate fate was a reality.

A knowledgeable Sherpa later spoke of the departure. "The men with them were the best we had. They were fearless, willing to go when no one else would. One told me the white man, Derek, was trembling. Something was very wrong. He thought that witch, Tarja, had put a curse on him. They talked about coming back, but if they had, no one would ever have hired them again."

A few moments after Crystal gave up on the interview, Derek set out with his team, neglecting to wave back at the camera. Ten minutes later, the second team stepped off.

Below, the clouds filled the canyons, sweeping in a billowing mass toward distant Nepal. The sky above was layered with a thin veneer of gray clouds. It was as if the expedition was cut off from the world and existed in its own barren mountain kingdom.

Tarja had been told to return to Advanced Base Camp, but had given no indication of her intentions, though it was taken that was what she was going to do. To everyone's surprise, she set out with Team One. A few yards from the camp, the team stopped and Reggie confronted her.

"Tarja, go back. I told you last night," he said.

"It was agreed we'd summit together. Now get out of my way."

"Things have changed. You know that. Now go back before you get hurt."

"Are you threatening me?" she demanded.

"Of course not. But you aren't welcome. Go back. Please."

Derek stepped up. "Go back down, Tarja. Do as you're told for once."

"Go to hell, Derek. If you'd kept it in your zipper, none of this would be happening. Now I'm going to summit. Period." She set off and, a few minutes later, Team One resumed its climb.

Tarja was clearly determined to summit no matter what her husband told her. After that, no words were exchanged between the Team One climbers and the Nordic beauty. Reggie led the way and set a brutal pace, perhaps hoping that the woman would drop out. In the end, all struggled to one degree or another as they moved toward Camp Three and Tarja doggedly maintained the pace.

Climbing from Advanced Base Camp to Camp Three, the ice was uncommonly slick and the way was treacherous. The climbers carefully planted their crampons to keep from falling on a long patch of blue ice. The stiff wind made the climb even more difficult in these conditions as the climbers were forced to brace themselves against it. Most of all, however, the wind kept them cold—even as they moved without pause up the side of the mountain.

Slipping along this route was deadly. Every hundred feet or so, it was necessary for each climber to remove their clip from the line and reconnect it past the anchor. In their numbed state and robotic mindset, it was possible to miss the line entirely and falsely believe that they were securely connected. Every season someone made this mistake and paid the price.

This is a different kind of climbing for the twenty-first century. Since time immemorial—certainly since the conquest of the Matterhorn and the invention of Alpine style climbing—it has been the practice of climbers to connect one to the other. Should a climber fall, the others in a more secure position were able to save him from death. The system was not foolproof. Sometimes it was possible for a single climber to fall, pulling the others with him, taking the entire line to their death.

For this reason, climbers always make certain of the capability of the other climbers because their lives depend on it. This is the reason climbers have always shared a close friendship and camaraderie one with the other. Climbers who do not normally get along—even climbers who are otherwise antagonists—are brothers on the mountain. Everyone's life depends on the ability of the other.

However, this is not the case on Everest. Since climbers are not roped to each other, there is no reason for them to be satisfied with the abilities of the other climbers. And because of the line, climbers of acceptable physical ability—but with very limited climbing skills—routinely tackle the giant. The result is that climbers don't trust each other. The bond between climbers simply doesn't exist. Because the expert climbs beside the newcomer, the kind of kinship that is historically commonplace among mountaineers is eliminated.

Today the Sherpa string line from Base Camp along the entire route the climbers follow, all the way to the highest point on earth. Should they fall, in most cases, they will not die. Only a gross mistake, such as failing to connect to the line, can cause them to fall to their deaths, though in recent years the crowding has been such that literally a hundred climbers are attached to a relatively short stretch of line. Should a few of those take a tumble, they could potentially bring down everyone. It is only a question of time.

In fact, it is said that even a reasonably fit man or woman could climb Everest since it takes no great technical skill. For that reason, reasonably fit climbers with no special skills flock to Everest. There is a full measure of contempt from skilled climbers when they encounter the comfortably rich amateurs with whom they will climb. It is easy to understand why so many climbers pass by other fallen climbers in need of their help.

The line has brought a greater measure of security to Everest climbing. Avalanches, which cannot be controlled, the crossing of chasms, exhaustion, and the various diseases of high altitude kill climbers on Everest.

―――

As the teams moved up the sheet of ice and frozen snow, they came upon recurring reminders of their peril. Between Camp Two and Camp Three they passed several bodies frozen to the ice, some of them dating back more than two decades. Some were as recent as the previous season.

One of the peculiarities of climbing Everest is this lack of reaction to the bodies of dead climbers. Encounter a body anywhere else on earth and nearly anyone would be shocked. They would be concerned about what had happened. There would be a desire that the body be treated with respect. In most cases, whatever you had planned would be placed on hold while you saw to the dead body.

These bodies litter the summit approaches like so much confetti and are taken just as casually. Climbers turn aside their gazes and move steadily beyond the dead—and often the dying—oblivious that this could be their fate in a few short hours.

There is no respect for the dead on Everest. People remain where they die and, on the windswept stretches of the mountain, bodies can remain visible for decades. At the sheltered camps, a layer of snow and ice builds up each year. The result is that new tents are erected atop the bodies of the dead. It has been said that you can climb from Base Camp to the summit on the bodies of the dead.

The reality is that with an oxygen-starved brain and a determination to climb the mountain, no living climber has a moment of compassion for the fallen. There is, in fact, no consideration that it could be themselves lying there. There is no thought for the families of the dead. No recovery of personal effects. No effort even to attempt to identify the dead. They are simply passed without consideration, without a prayer. Only on Everest are the dead considered a natural part of the terrain.

"They disrespect the dead," a Sherpa says. "The ghosts of those who died are still there because their body has not been treated with respect, the proper prayers said. At night, we Sherpa hear them wailing their anguish. When we tell the Westerners about it so they will be better, they laugh. They tell us we are superstitious, that it is only the wind."

Who can say?

Peer is widely regarded as the greatest mountain climber in the world. In Europe, he is a household name. His smiling face appears from time to time on the cover of every major magazine. We can only speculate about what was on his mind as they set out. He should have been climbing Everest with the best, within a cocoon of security only the truly expert can provide. Instead, he was plodding his way up the mountain with a pair of squabbling spouses, serving as point man on an expedition that was little more than a publicity stunt.

After him, the most expert climber was Derek or more likely Reggie. However, none of these were as good as the Sherpa, who are born climbers. They set about their task with grim determination. They'd seen tough times before and would see this through, the gods willing.

The two teams made steady, exhausting, progress above Advanced Base Camp. Derek was clearly struggling and often stopped to hold his side.

The way of climbing is well established—except for the Sherpa who are the most fit. This was, after all, their domain. Each climber placed his left foot in front of him, then his right foot. He then stopped to breathe three or four breaths, and then repeats the process: left foot, right foot, breath. And so it continues without rest, without stopping, until they reach the next camp.

Along the way, lungs burn with an icy fire. Each climber must force himself to drink, since it's easy to become dehydrated. No one has an appetite. Above Base Camp, climbers lose weight steadily. Above Advanced Base Camp, the body is consuming itself. In the Death Zone that begins just above Camp Four, the body is positively devouring itself.

The climbers might hear an occasional word from one of the other climbers, but primarily all they hear is their own heavy breathing or the coughing of another climber. None of them would waste any effort on speech. It was tedious, inglorious labor.

From below, the climb was monitored by telescope. In his bright orange high-altitude climbing suit, Derek was easily spotted in even the most deadly of places. He was—they say of him that day—a fearless climber.

# How Mt. Everest is Destroying the Sherpa

*By Alaap Sajan*
*Sherpa News*
*June 2*

To the Sherpa, the highest point on earth is Sagarmatha, the mother goddess. For centuries, they have worshiped at her flanks. Today, young Sherpa men stand in line to become highly paid guides up those very flanks—the majesty and awe the mountain once inspired, all but vanished.

Despite civil war and social unrest, one link in the Nepal economy that has flourished in both good times and bad has been the climbing industry. It is estimated that as many as 9,000 Nepalese, mostly Sherpa, are engaged by the various foreign expeditions that come here every year. Though several mountains are attractive, the single greatest target of this interest is Mt. Everest.

Girija Lama, executive director of the Sherpa Foundation, laments that all this attention on one target is slowly destroying traditional Sherpa culture. "The Sherpa have seen a steady decline in all aspects of their existence since this mad rush to climb Mt. Everest began. No sooner does a Sherpa save a bit of money, than he takes his family to Kathmandu where their identity as Sherpa comes to an abrupt end."

Mr. Lama says the damage to those who remain in the traditional Sherpa villages is nearly as devastating. "Successful guides take many wives, which disrupts the normal pattern of village existence. Jealously, once unknown among the gentle Sherpa, is now epidemic." In addition, young boys increasingly disdain the traditional livelihoods of the village and instead train to become guides some day.

"It may already be too late to save the Sherpa culture," Mr. Lama said.

# Chapter Six
# Into the Death Zone

Even with the bracing wind and freezing cold, the struggling Derek and Team One arrived at Camp Four on the South Col as scheduled. Team Two held back despite the blistering pace.

The scene upon arrival was not one of harmony. Absent was the usual camaraderie of climbers bonded by their assault on the world's highest mountain, in the world's most deadly locale. Instead, Reggie confronted Tarja again—even before she set foot in the camp. He was now enraged that Derek's wife had disobeyed him and moved up the mountain rather than descending as she'd been told.

"You're not welcome here," Reggie said. "Your husband has made that clear enough. You cannot continue without help. You must turn back. You have no choice unless you really intend to die up here."

"Don't you tell me what to do," she retorted. "I know my husband better than you. He doesn't mean what he says. It's important we summit together. He understands that. I'll talk to him. You'll see."

But Derek refused to meet with his wife, though it was a small place and there was really nowhere for him to escape to. He turned his back and pretended that he didn't hear as she implored him. It was humiliating for both of them. Tarja kept moving around to face him, but Derek moved to keep his back to her. She'd exhaust herself in effort, bend at her waist, cough, and hack, before starting up again.

Finally, Peer stepped in and led her away, cooing softly into her ear and telling her that there was nothing to be done. The wind was gusting and no one heard what she said in reply. Her attempt in the end to stomp off in anger looked childish in the conditions.

An exhausted Derek was now joined by Rusty, who'd stayed out of the fiasco. He shot a few minutes of scenery followed by a brief clip of Derek smiling bravely against the backdrop of Everest. Tarja, who had nowhere to go on the small campsite, watched, enraged when Rusty failed to direct the camera toward her. At one point, she approached him, demanding that he film her.

"Listen," she said, "you're employed by the Sodoc expedition. Derek is going to change his mind. You'll see. This is only a tiff. You just need to do what you're told. Now point the camera at me and let me give you an interview."

Instead, Rusty directed the camera to the snow at his feet. "Derek's my boss," he said, "not you. It's clear enough you're not supposed to be here. I have my instructions."

Tarja said more, but it made no difference. Rusty had seen combat in the first Gulf War and over the years had climbed some of the world's tallest peaks. He'd faced death any number of times. He was not a man to be intimidated by the likes of the mattress-hopping Tarja—no matter how tough she talked.

Afterward, the teams rested as best they could for what little remained of the day. There was little shelter except in or beside the small tents. Everest loomed above them, drawing them like a magnet. Though unspoken, its commanding presence served as a reminder to every climber of the possibility of death.

By all accounts, the climbers were not in good condition. All of them were coughing badly. During the late afternoon, the freezing breeze turned limbs numb. No one ate. All they could manage was a bit of hot sweet tea.

The still-angry Tarja had crawled into a tent. The others clustered about Reggie as he used a sat telephone to check the weather and announced that the wind was expected to ease overnight. Both teams welcomed the news. Reggie added, "The bad news, unfortunately, is that there is an approaching front. It looks to be a nasty one."

"When will it reach the summit?" Peer asked. Derek was oddly quiet.

"It's not anticipated for another seventy-two hours," Reggie said. "That gives us just enough time to summit and get back down. But these patterns are unpredictable. I've seen them slow to a crawl with no force at all by the time they reach the mountain. And I've seen them race well ahead of schedule. I believe that nowhere else on earth is the weather less predictable and more deadly than where we are now standing. I want all of you to think about that from this point on. Derek, you should give serious thought to returning to ABC tomorrow to wait this out. I have word that the team climbing above us is turning back, while the one below us plans to retreat tomorrow. They don't want to take any chances and I agree with them. We can tackle this in a few days."

Derek shook his head. "So much the better for us if the route is clear above. We aren't going back down. That's final. Everyone needs to accept that we are committed. There's too much riding on this for me to retreat."

Such was his state of mind on that second-to-last day of his life. You can be rich, famous, handsome, and have all the breaks in life, but on Everest, you're just another climber. When it's your time, there's nothing to be done about it—especially when so-called friends, those sycophants and hangers-on who've put you in this predicament, turn their backs and leave you to die.

Reggie appeared to want to say more, but refrained. Then he addressed the teams. "In that event, a clock must be running in all your thoughts. You have only a limited amount of time, a few short hours on this mountain at this altitude. Pay attention to the weather. Remember, it doesn't count if you don't get back alive."

It is possible to be part of an Everest expedition and never confront the enormity of what lies ahead. Climbers can trek to Base Camp—even encounter obstacles along the way—and still not understand what awaits them. They can struggle with the acclimatization and their own personal medical needs and still not confront honestly why they are there. But they cannot reach Camp Four and spend a miserable night freezing and cold with that ominous, overhanging presence without knowing that they are soon about to step into the abyss.

It was a night of lonely thoughts. Each climber was on the mountain for his or her own reasons and in those hours surely came to terms with them. Derek was there as part of a life plan only he understood, assuming that he even did. Tarja was there to receive the glow from her husband's fame and move up the international celebrity ladder.

The Sherpa, Reggie, and Peer were there because they were paid and because this is what they did. Without the mountain, they would have been less than they were. Any other life was unthinkable for them.

But why was Scott in that desolate place? Reportedly it was because his friend Derek asked him, but, unlike the others, Scott was not an adventurer. Until this expedition, he'd never voiced an interest in climbing Everest. He told others on the trek that he only intended to go to Base Camp. Later, he insisted that he would go no higher than Advanced Base Camp. Yet here he was at Camp Four. Later, given the opportunity, he never explained himself. He has never justified his actions.

You can only ask yourself *why*.

~~~

The climbers attempted to sleep in high-altitude jumpsuits inside their sleeping bags. Each of them was cold to their bones. Not far from where they tossed were the bodies of three dead climbers—one of them partially exposed in an abandoned tent not fifteen feet from the center of their small campsite. Only by averting their eyes or within the blanket of night could they fail to see the danger they were in.

To allow any sleep at all—any rest that allowed reserves of strength and endurance to remain fixed if not rebuild—each slept with a bottle of oxygen. Still, sleep largely evaded even the most intrepid.

All of them, even Derek, were at the entry point to the Death Zone. From this spot on, no one climbed without the aid of oxygen. Even the Sherpa with their enlarged hearts, oversized lungs, and fierce determination, used oxygen. It is true that they can get to the summit without it, but not without enormous effort and—even then—many of them die. The number of Westerners who have reached the summit of Everest without oxygen can be counted on the fingers of two hands. These are extraordinary men.

For the rest of us normal beings, oxygen is essential. Even the great George Mallory took oxygen with him on that last deadly day. Sir Edmund Hillary also used oxygen. Oxygen is the elixir of life in the Death Zone, but it is no guarantee that a climber will escape death.

Above Camp Four, a climber's time is measured in hours. The flow of oxygen from the mask does not return him to the amount he is actually adapted to despite all the acclimatization. It restores his oxygen level only to that of Camp One above Base Camp, which means that he is still receiving just half the amount of oxygen his body demands. Acclimatization, with its increase in corpuscles, compensates for some of the lack. But neither supplemental oxygen nor an increased blood count provides enough oxygen at these altitudes. They make climbing Everest possible—but only barely so.

From Camp Four to the summit is like being on Mars. It's bitterly cold, lacking enough oxygen to survive, windswept, and isolated. There is no possibility of outside intervention. No helicopter can fly this high. Even if one could, there's nowhere to land.

The only help a climber can reasonably expect comes from within. Those reservoirs of strength and courage that have carried him this far can, in extremity, mean the difference between life and death. More than one climber given up for dead has risen as if from an icy grave to find his way down the mountain. Far more, however, disappear or turn into those frozen colorful lumps other climbers pass without comment.

If a climber is very, very lucky, the other climbers with him are strong enough and motivated enough to help if he's in trouble. After all, that's why they are there. You have those you've paid, in essence, to save your life. Often you have fellow climbers you trust. Derek had each of these, but he also had men he believed to be friends—men he believed would extend the same last measure of devotion he'd give them if the roles were reversed.

The reality of Everest is that the mountain sucks the vitality from even the healthiest and heartiest of men. It takes extraordinary will to help another when you feel yourself so at risk—friend, client, or not. At least, that's the excuse.

Regardless, the result is that people die above Camp Four. That's the consequence of stepping into the Death Zone; it is also the allure. Everest is one of the last places on earth where you cannot be saved from yourself. There is no seatbelt, shoulder strap, or airbag to save you in an accident. There is no parachute when leaping from the burning airplane. There is no bungee connected to this jump. You have stepped into the deadly unknown; you have cast your dice in the world's most lethal game.

---

At first light, the climbers stirred in their tents. Each pair lit their own feeble flame to heat water for tea and to brew porridge if eating was possible. The climbers emerged from their small tents still exhausted from their efforts the previous day and groggy from lack of sleep.

This was the end—one way or the other—for they were all but on summit day. God willing, they'd move up to the bivouac known as Camp Five where they'd spend a few hours attempting rest, breathing oxygen. At midnight, this same day, they would suit up and set out for the summit. The final day of the climb would end in triumph or tragedy.

As the men buckled themselves into their climbing gear, Reggie, who'd spent the night in the tent with him, took Derek aside for another attempt to turn him back. "I've talked to Calvin by sat phone. You need to go back down. We can do this again in a week or ten days. There's still time."

Derek smiled wanly. "It's now or never. They're depending on me to deliver the goods."

"I've seen how you hold your side. You moved very slowly yesterday. It only gets worse from here."

"We're on gas now. It will be better. I had a good night."

"The hell you did. You were wheezing and coughing all night. I doubt you slept more than five minutes in any one stretch. It's early in the season yet. There will be other periods of summit weather. You have to listen to me."

"Father won't like it," Derek said. "The network has a schedule and I've got to keep it."

About then, Tarja emerged from her tent along with Peer, who'd spent the night with her. Once again, she attempted to speak to Derek, but he refused. Finally, Reggie blocked her from him, telling her she had to turn back.

"I will not go back down the mountain!" she shouted.

"You have no choice. We will give you no help from this point on. I have instructed the Sherpa and none of them will aid you in any way. You cannot be so foolish as to go on alone because alone you will die. That's simply how it is. Go back!"

"Derek!" she shouted. "Derek!" But her husband ignored her. "Scott! Peer! Do something!"

The men just shook their heads. She'd made no friends with them—even if she had given her body to Peer. Plus, they knew who buttered their bread. As the climbers finished readying themselves, realization and acceptance of her predicament slowly dawned on Tarja. She has had few disappointments in her life. There was an odd moment as Tarja took Peer aside and spoke to him in feverish whispers. No one knows what she said or, to be more exact, no one who knows is saying. At one point, Peer looked up, stared directly at Derek, and slowly nodded his head in apparent comprehension.

Within minutes, Tarja finished preparing her gear. "You're all bastards!" she shouted at the cluster of men. She paused at the edge of the camp and glared at the climbers as the first of the teams set out for Camp Five. "I hope you all die! You shits!" Then she left, alone, to descend back down the mountain. Rusty never once pointed his camera at her.

~~~

The teams left five minutes apart, but they soon formed a single ragged line, their brightly colored high-altitude jumpsuits stark against the pale white of Everest. Reggie had been right; Derek struggled all day. Peer led the way with Team Two, but was forced to stop from time and time to avoid overtaking Team One.

Because of the slow pace, Rusty was able to struggle ahead of the climbers and film them making their laborious way up the mountain. Any shots of the struggling Derek were meant to be cut later. Instead, we would all see the tragedy after word of his death swept across the world.

Though they were on oxygen, the climb to Camp Five was scarcely better than the climb had been the day before. All of them were coughing; all of them were exhausted. Sources say that there was little talk among themselves and almost no communication with the camp below.

Crystal was filming with a telephoto lens from ABC; Derek's struggle was clearly apparent even at that distance. Communication on the radio was not secure, so the climbers had agreed to a form of code. She called repeatedly to ask Derek how he was. He answered that he was fine only the first time. After that, Reggie responded since Derek was too exhausted and out of breath to speak.

Three hours into the ascent, the teams encountered the Nepalese expedition retreating down the mountain. The teams paused to exchange thoughts. "Too risky," Girija told them. "It's unhealthy up there and the weather's turning nasty. Bad weather is on the way. Don't be foolish."

In his BBC interview, Girija described the scene. "Mr. Sodoc looked very ill. Many of us were quite sick as well. There had been an unusual amount of illness that year. Who can say why? But what we told them was the truth. The weather was closing in very fast. No man should have continued that day."

Asked about reports that his team had tampered with the lines: "Slander is what it is."

At four o'clock that afternoon, the two teams of the Sodoc expedition reached Camp Five and took possession of the tents that had been erected by their Sherpa. Reggie used the sat phones to check the weather and then called a meeting. The climbers clustered together on the leeward side of one of the tents. Every man looked exhausted.

"I'm glad to say that the front is moving as predicted," Reggie said. "It's due tomorrow night. Everyone needs to be back to Camp Four before nightfall tomorrow. Plan your turnaround point accordingly. Do you understand?"

The climbers all acknowledged him.

"The schedule is still going according to plan. If all goes well, you should summit around noon tomorrow. You can expect to pass through Camp Five between two and three in the afternoon and be at Camp Four before dark. If you must, stay here—though I much prefer you make Camp Four. Just don't get caught any higher up."

Such was the plan.

It was early afternoon as the climbers brewed tea. Peer managed to eat a PowerBar, but no one else consumed food. Afterward, though it was still light, everyone settled in for the night.

By now Tarja had reached Advanced Base Camp, bitching to anyone who would listen about being forced to descend alone and how no one would help her. She was an object of amusement—especially for the Sherpa who had always found her behavior bizarre and disliked having women so far up the mountain.

"They drain the life force from a man," a Sherpa told me. "They are weak and take what power they have from men. On the mountain, a man only has so much power. He has none to give a woman. They are demons that high up and can only cause death."

Tarja snatched a satellite phone from Crystal and called her agent in New York. It was by all accounts an unpleasant telephone call. Just what Tarja thought her agent could do half the planet away, she has never explained.

To say the whole world knew about the summit attempt is an exaggeration. But in the United States and Europe, the coverage reached saturation as the media campaign reached fever pitch. It was impossible to be near a television set or radio or to browse the Internet and not know that Derek was about to climb Mt. Everest. Every aspect of the expedition had been lavishly covered and this final act was no exception.

Except it was all a lie.

There was no happily married couple about to climb the highest point on earth—and Derek was not making good progress up the mountain. He was sick and injured. He was not surrounded by faithful companions. But the public knew none of this.

Derek's friends should have insisted that he turned back. There are times to intervene with those you care about—and this was one of them. But no one did. No one cared, not really.

Peer and Scott were skilled Alpinists who had never climbed Everest and were determined to summit. Doc Cal was too far down the mountain to effectively use his influence. Reggie was too weak-willed to tell a paying client that he was in no shape to continue.

It was a perfect storm of human indifference and selfishness.

The world watched a sanitized version of events. Instead, Derek tried to rest—sleep even—in his cold sleeping bag. He lay in pain, shivering and miserable, driven by a desire to please his father—and whatever personal demons we can only imagine.

# Why Amateurs Risk It All to Climb Everest

*The Everest* blog
Posted June 9

It is a little known fact that, until recent years, only highly skilled climbers attempted the highest point on earth. Today, it seems, every reasonably fit man or woman with some money makes the attempt. It has turned into a sort of cottage industry and in no small measure that is why so many amateurs are dying up there.

Skilled Sherpa guides do all of the heavy lifting and, even above Base Camp, climbers retain a measure of convenience, even luxury, not normally associated with high-altitude climbing. The administering of modern drugs makes success more likely than ever. The Sherpa have also been known to short-rope an exhausted climber to, in effect, pull them to the summit. All the climber is required to do is stay afoot.

Mt. Everest is the Holy Grail for climbers and their motive is clear enough as they jockey for position to have their photograph taken on the summit. A successful climb assures a lifetime of bragging rights.

Of course, an unsuccessful climb often adds to the growing body count.

# Chapter Seven

# An Icy Embrace

Shortly before midnight, the climbers stirred in their tents. The lights inside cast a pale silver glow in the darkness, lighting the tents like stark oriental lanterns. After a bit of tea, each man emerged slowly into the bitter cold and darkness.

Every climber—Sherpa and Westerner alike—checked his gear and prepared for the big push. All wore headlamps to light their way, resembling miners in the black night. Each also wore a radio and microphone so they could communicate one with one another and with Doc Cal and Crystal.

The wind had at last stopped. It remained cold, but not as fiercely cold as it had been the previous day. Derek was the last climber to prepare. He was very sick and coughed repeatedly. Reggie could be heard speaking into his ear, attempting to get him to turn back, but Derek refused. His competitive nature and drive had utterly consumed him. He would summit—or he would die trying.

When it was apparent that Team Two was ready, Reggie spoke to Peer and Scott. "Go on ahead," he told them. "The Nepalese turned back, so no one's been above for several days and there was a storm earlier. Check the lines and make certain they are secured. Peer, clear the route as needed. We will follow you in a little while."

Team Two, eager to be on their way, left without a second thought. Their headlamps cast a pale light on the ice and snow as they moved slowly away, then up the mountain.

It was nearly an hour before Team One finally left. Derek was in very, very bad shape. Shockingly, he'd already consumed his entire allotment of Decadron and was given more. Whatever effect Diamox was having had reached its limit. Now he was popping Decadron for prophylactic relief. It was a dangerous situation.

This was the culmination of a massive media event—more akin to the coverage of a traveling circus than to real news. Nearly one hundred years before, it had been observed that when you climb Everest, you cannot be of two minds. You cannot combine a scientific with a climbing expedition. On Everest all of your effort and energy must be devoted to the climb iteself. The sole object must be to put the man on top.

The Sodoc expedition violated the most basic rule of climbing Everest—at least as much energy was spent on covering the climb and manufacturing stories as was spent reaching the top. Divided purposes elsewhere often result in failure. It is no different on Everest—except there failure means death.

Since setting out, Rusty had filmed at every opportunity. Crystal received his feeds, gave them a rough edit, and sent them on to New York for airing, while in some cases entire segments aired live. Breathless reports were filed every few hours. SNS had three reporters blogging constantly, issuing Internet press releases, and drumming up interest. Anchors in New York, London, and Paris delivered updates every half hour. Remember Pearl Harbor and the first moonwalk, this was the same intensity of worldwide interest. Only the

Internet made it much larger. The world was watching as if it were Norgay and Hillary.

At this altitude, in these conditions, with every step up the mountain, a climber's mental condition deteriorated. By the time the teams reached 27,000 feet, their minds were exercising the judgment of a five-year-old child. One of the unspoken realities of Everest is the difficulty climbers experience in thinking clearly. Many die because they make bad decisions—decisions they would never make at sea level.

The moon had not risen and lamps were the only light marking the way. As if in a dream bypassing the extreme danger on either side of the light. Were they to become unattached from the line and slip, they would have fallen to their deaths.

Before dawn, Team Two reached the area known as the Balcony at 27,600 feet. The largest number of Mt. Everest photographs are snapped here. Nature's beauty abounds and surrounds you. But on this black night, there were no photographs.

Peer stopped and spoke into his mouthpiece. "Reggie, we're at the Balcony."

"Good job," came the reply.

Peer, Scott, and their two Sherpa guides could see the lights of Team One bobbing far below. "We can see you from here," Peer added, discreetly not mentioning the distance between the teams. Neither Peer nor Scott suggested waiting on Derek, whom they clearly knew needed their assistance. Peer had been hired to help and Derek was depending on Scott's friendship—but instead of waiting, they set out toward the summit.

"We're pushing off now," Peer said. "We'll link up shortly."

Below the Balcony, it was difficult going for Derek. To his credit, he struggled on, determined to reach the top of the world and fulfill his promises. As Team Two resumed its move up the mountain, it was unencumbered and they increased the distance between the two teams, making it more difficult for either to help the other. Below, sources say, Reggie tried repeatedly to convince Derek to turn back, but he steadfastly refused.

The rising sun found Team Two on the Southeast Ridge approaching the Hillary Step. With sunlight, the rising temperature began to soften the hard ice. The footing became less stable and more uncertain, though the sun was a welcome respite from the relentless cold.

To this point, Peer and the Sherpa had found the lines up the mountain to be secured. The passageway was also clear. As a result, Peer and Scott had little to do but climb. In the warmer air and sparkling sunlight, feeling slowly returned to numbed feet, hands, and cheeks.

They soon reached the Southeast Ridge at 27,800 feet. To the left was Nepal, while Tibet stretched vast and brown to the right. Even the slightest breeze swept across the ridge with force. In storms, climbers have been known to be completely blown off the ridge. But this morning the air was dead calm.

Again, neither Peer nor Scott gave any thought to waiting for Derek. Instead, they pressed on and by midmorning were at the South Summit, where they stopped to consider their situation. Peer called down. "We are at the South Summit, Reggie. Where are you?"

"We're still back. Wait there for us. We may need your assistance."

After a long pause, Peer said, "I disagree. It's not difficult to reach this point. Your lot can handle that. I think we should move on to Hillary Step. We don't know if the line to there is still in place. We don't know if the line up the Step is secure or even visible. It will take at least one hour to string another if we need to. We don't want to delay you when you get there."

After a long wait; Reggie reluctantly agreed since the Hillary Step line was essential. Derek's condition was not good and it was important to keep moving.

"We'll meet on the shelf above the Step," Peer said. With that, Team Two set out.

This was not what Reggie had meant. Surely he thought that Team One would wait below Hillary Step once they made certain that the line was in place or they had strung a new one. They could be of no use atop the difficult precipice.

Below them, Team Two could see patches of thin clouds within a light mist. They could see the West Ridge up to Pumori and further across Cho Oyu's white peak—the sixth highest mountain in the world. However, this was no time for scenery.

It was a short distance for Team Two to the bottom of the Hillary Step. As it was, the line was secure and it was no great difficulty for the four men to scramble to the top, with Peer taking the lead. They were now just an hour from the peak and summit fever once again consumed them. Thought of rendering assistance to their struggling friend had now firmly taken a back seat.

On the shelf, they stopped and rested—even pushing back their masks and setting aside the microphones so they could speak in private to one another. What they said and what they planned is known only to them. We judge their words from their behavior.

The men were exhausted. We should not pretend it was otherwise. They were not Superman. It takes an extraordinary physical effort and great discipline to climb so high. But there can be no question that Scott and Peer, as well as the two Sherpa, were elated. In an hour, they could be on the summit of Everest—that is, if they pushed on and didn't wait.

Of the four men, only one of the Sherpa had stood at the top of the world before. Courageous as Peer was, as well known as he is in Europe, and for all of his remarkable accomplishments, he had never previously climbed as high. For that matter, neither had the other Sherpa, who had no idea that he would be dead within a few hours.

Scott, of course, says that he never intended to climb Everest. He claims that he only went on the expedition at Derek's request. Judge for yourself.

Below in Advanced Base Camp, Crystal was expressing her concern. With their code, she and Rusty could speak honestly and he had conveyed to her over the radio the true status of Team One. She knew that Derek was struggling. She turned to Doc Cal and said, "Do you want to try to talk him down?"

Doc Cal shook his head. "I tried earlier and did no good."

"What are we going to do?" she said.

"I'm going to move up to Camp Four in the morning with two Sherpa and prepare to meet them on their way down. In the event that they do turn back today, I will move up to meet them—even if it's dark. Derek isn't listening to common sense. I don't know what else we can do." Then he added, "He's a fine athlete. He has plenty of help from both experts and friends. He'll be all right. You'll see."

At SNS headquarters in New York, there was no concern for Derek's safety. The suits were preoccupied with the timing of the summit. It was anticipated that Derek would broadcast from the top of the world for breakfast news broadcasts in the United Kingdom and Europe. They had considered asking him to summit at five in the afternoon to catch the evening news broadcast on the American East Coast. But when informed that Derek would need to come down the mountain in the dark and that climbers who attempted a nighttime descent nearly always died, they changed their mind.

We can assume that the senior Sodoc was glued to his plasma screens. Derek was, after all, his only son. And even though Derek was not active in the management of the company, surely Michael Sodoc believed that he could eventually persuade his son to assume the reins of his media empire. He wanted no harm to come to him.

In the meantime, Team One gamely struggled up the mountain. By this time, Derek could scarcely move. With each step, he was compelled to stop and suck air into his burning lungs before attempting another.

The sole survivor of Team One isn't talking, but it's not difficult to imagine what was happening. Moving at such a slow pace, surely they were all very cold. Reggie spoke to Derek regularly, to encourage him or to try to convince him to give up. Everyone was exhausted; Derek repeatedly refused to turn back.

And why should he? He was young and conditioned. He'd trained, directly and indirectly, for this moment for years. He'd already stood astride the other six highest points on earth. Even with his difficulties, there was no reason to believe that he would not succeed this day. He'd faced obstacles in the past and always overcome them. Other climbers in his condition have managed to summit and returned alive. He had no reason to believe that it would not be the same for him. After all, he had the very best in technology and excellent communications. He had the finest guide and the best climbing Sherpa. But most of all, he had friends he could trust an men he depended on.

And so he bore his misery, willing each foot in front of the other, and pressed on, certain in the knowledge that he was in good hands.

-----

At the shelf above Hillary Step, Derek's trusted friends were coming to a very different decision about their role that day. Admittedly, it's difficult to stay warm on Everest unless you move. Stand still long enough and you freeze solid. The four men remained in the sun, stamping their feet, their backs to the steady wind beating against them from the valleys below.

After a bit, Peer called down to Reggie. "What's the situation?" he asked.

There was a pause. "We're moving," Reggie answered.

"It's freezing up here."

"Where are you?" Reggie asked.

"On the shelf."

There was a pause, then, "What are you doing up there?"

"The line was secure. We moved up to test it," Peer said.

"I didn't know you planned to do that."

"It seemed right at the time. How long do we wait?"

"I'm not sure."

Now the reality of human nature asserted itself. Scott turned to Peer and said, "I didn't come this far only to turn back. You can tell Derek's not going to make it. We don't have a lot of time. I'm taking the Sherpa and moving up. You can wait here if you want."

"We should wait, Scott," Peer said. "We promised Derek we would help. You can't just set out on your own."

To climb Everest is to dance with death. How many decisions and non-decisions kill someone? The list is endless. It's reckless to go unprepared or in the wrong weather. It's murder to abandon a climber who can still be saved. But on Everest, there are rarely witnesses—except for God and He's not saying.

"I'm going," Scott repeated. "If you want to stay here and die, that's your business."

There it was. Despite any previous assumptions, this wasn't really about being of service to Derek. Keep in mind that all of their expenses were being paid and that every man had committed to helping Derek get to the summit. They'd given their word.

Consider that it was possible for them to see Team One below. Team Two knew how far away they were. Just as surely, they knew Team One needed help. They should have gone back down the Step they should never have climbed. They should have waited below to extend a helping hand. Instead, Scott made the decision to climb to the top.

Reluctantly, uncertain Derek would even get up Hillary Step, Peer joined the Sherpa and Scott as they began the final climb to the peak.

It was half an hour to cross the treacherous traverse from Hillary Step to the Summit Ridge. More than one climber has lost his life in the attempt and here, of all places, the line can be less certain. In bad weather, darkness, or a state of exhaustion, no stretch of rock on earth is more deadly. But uninjured, in the prime of life, and in perfect weather, it can be managed with little difficulty. Scott held back to let Peer lead the way and perform the difficult task of clearing away fresh snow. That placed him at the lead so it was Peer, a half hour later, who reached the summit first.

The first team to summit each year typically finds the summit mound crowned with virgin snow. Occasionally, a metal flagpole or two from the previous year can be seen partially bent, but more often than not, the summit is as pristine as the day it was when Hillary first stepped there. However, almost immediately, climbers turn the summit into a garbage dump. Refuse is thrown about at random, items are abandoned, and prayer flags are left behind. It becomes an unsightly place.

You would think that climbers would treat such a desired spot with more dignity. The Sherpa say, in part, that it is the disrespect Westerners show for the mountain that causes so many to die. Who are we to argue with that?

As Peer reached the summit, two teams of climbers were already there, having come up from the Tibet side of the mountain. There was a party atmosphere, as there often is. Not much later Scott and the other Sherpa arrived.

Everyone was eager to have his or her photograph taken and cameras were passed about. Climbers removed their oxygen masks and lifted their goggles so that their faces could be seen clearly in the photographs that they would hang on the wall. Everyone forced a smile—no matter how exhausted or sick they actually felt.

Some climbers simply collapsed at the top, utterly exhausted by the effort it had taken to get here. They slumped back against the snow looking very much like the dead. Many of them were in fact the walking dead. Having exhausted themselves, they had used every bit of energy to reach this goal, forgetting the most basic rule of climbing. Reaching the summit is the halfway point—not the goal.

There were approximately fifteen climbers at the top of the mountain at noon that day. Of those, seven would be dead in the next few hours—the beginning of the most deadly day in Everest history. The front so carefully tracked by the latest satellites refused to follow its predicted path or schedule. It did not care if men and women were exposed on the mountain or cut off from shelter and help. It was a mindless force that would expand itself as nature dictated. On this deadly day, the front gathered momentum and moved relentlessly toward the summit at a frightening speed.

As the celebration continued above, with great determination and grit Team One reached the foot of the Hillary Step. It had not been easy. At one point, a Sherpa was short-roped to Derek and essentially pulled him up the mountain.

Tsongba later said that at the Step, Reggie tried once again to talk Derek out of climbing up. But Derek was nearly to the top in his mind and it was only just noon—plenty of time to reach the summit and get back down. So he insisted. Under instructions, Rusty and the Sherpa moved up the Step to the shelf to film the moment when Derek would come up.

It was difficult getting Derek up that pitch of rock and ice. Tsongba says that he and Reggie all but carried him up. From above, at the halfway point, Rusty tossed down a line and he and the Sherpa helped pull Derek to the top. It was slow, exhausting work. It took more than an hour, but finally all of the men were on the shelf—a mere hour from their objective in normal conditions and reasonably fit health. But as a chain that is no stronger than its weakest link, Team One could move no faster than its slowest climber and its total life force was no greater than its most feeble climber.

Once he'd gathered his breath, Derek turned to Rusty and said, "I want you to move across the traverse so you can film me as I come over. I don't want shots of me from behind." He then moved to a wall of rock out of the wind where he leaned, holding his side, inhaling oxygen as he tried to rest. After a few minutes, Rusty and one of the Sherpa hooked themselves to the line and moved across the traverse to the Summit Ridge, where they stood waiting.

The scene was now set for disaster. It is said of Everest that simple decisions become hard and casual mistakes become lethal. "This was lunacy," a knowledgeable source says. "Reggie was letting a very sick man make life-and-death decisions for all of them. It is no wonder so many died."

Team Two was on the summit of Everest—too distant to give any help and Team One was now divided. Rusty was waiting on the far side of the traverse with a Sherpa. Derek, Tsongba, Reggie, and another Sherpa were on the shelf, unmoving.

What happened next is a mystery—calculated, I might add, to remain one. We know for a fact that Derek never left the shelf. This was his grave. All the money, all the energy, and all the media focus culminated in nothing more than getting him to his own grave.

Derek and the others remained—essentially unmoving—waiting for what we don't know and all froze to death except for Tsongba. We can assume that Derek was unable to continue and either unwilling or unable to retreat. There was no communication from the shelf to Advanced Base Camp during those final minutes when such communication was possible. At such an elevation, time passes like sand through your fingers and can never be recaptured.

Finally, for reasons never explained, Rusty and a Sherpa stopped waiting. We can assume that they realized Derek wasn't coming. If we want to be extraordinarily fair-minded, we can take that Rusty was moving to the summit to film shots that he could use later in the show about Derek's triumph. Maybe that's what he told himself. Others say it was summit fever. Regardless of his reasons, the two men set out for the peak without Derek.

Now the storm struck with all its fury. Blinding snow and freezing wind enveloped every climber like an icy blanket. A temperature already at zero now plunged to thirty below, with a wind chill factor even lower than that. Within moments of the blizzard striking, Reggie sent his first distress call.

"Scott, Rusty, Peer—we need you back here on the shelf. Please respond."

Since the introduction of radios on Everest, analog radios have been the standard. These are the same radios that first responders have used for decades. They are intended to work inside vehicles and buildings. For all of their strengths, however, they have enormous shortcomings. For one, they suffer from a short battery life. Their range is also limited. And with too much interference, the signal is weak or breaks up.

In recent years, they have been replaced with digital radios. These have great advantages. The battery life is significantly extended and they have a wider range. Their signal is strong and clear. But their one great shortcoming is that they are primarily line-of-sight. If an obstacle stands between radios, one cannot speak to the other. And with digital radios, the signal is either perfect or nonexistent.

Neither type of radio is ideal on Everest. Both are subject to malfunction. Both can be battered about until they no longer work. Most of all, their batteries cease to function if they get too cold—as it was on this day. An hour after the temperature plummeted, every radio stopped working. The climbers were all cut off from one another. No one heard Reggie from then on.

There are standards of behavior for climbers in such situations. From the south, there is only one way to the summit. The route is carefully marked because a line extends along it from Base Camp to the summit. Since climbers were always attached to the rope, the climber in trouble remains on the rope and cannot be missed. There is no reason to go searching because they are easily found and easily seen in normal situations.

When climbers have been lost, it is because they have disconnected themselves from the line and wandered away from the route. This has happened when the anchors have come loose and the line is blown down in a storm. On other occasions, climbers have decided to take a longer, gentler path down where possible, because someone is injured or they don't feel that they can stay on their feet if they take a steeper route. In such cases, climbers have become disoriented in a storm, lain down in the snow, and frozen to death. This is what happened to several of the climbers in 1996. The lesson is simple enough: stay on the line.

Now as the blizzard engulfed the climbers, those who could began to move down the mountain. Peer left the summit first, just before the storm struck, descending alone since he'd arrived first. Scott and the other Sherpa followed shortly thereafter and made their way slowly toward the shelf above Hillary Step. Engulfed in the blizzard, no one could speak to the others by radio. Every man hiked in his own silent cocoon.

The media buzz continued worldwide. Breathless anchors intoned their stories, relying on stock footage Crystal had provided. The paid bloggers blogged away. There was not the slightest hint of the climbers' deadly situation.

On the shelf, the situation was becoming desperate as the oxygen tanks ran low. Since the men were no longer moving, their body temperatures plummeted. They became increasingly cut off from their own bodies as limbs turned numb. The men clustered together for a time, seeking shelter from the storm, uttering words of encouragement. In time, Derek told the other three to leave and save themselves, but they refused. Instead, Reggie positioned himself in the storm to intercept help coming down from the mountain and was soon joined by Tsongba in a futile and tragic effort to save their client.

Peer, we know, was first off the traverse. Alone, he searched the shelf for the others, but could find no one. Determined and courageous, he continued, working blindly in the blizzard, disregarding his own safety until finally he encountered Tsongba, who had collapsed in the snow. Like a faithful horse, Sherpa are known to push themselves until they can endure no more. When they die on the mountain, death usually comes quickly as they have exhausted every ounce of their energy.

The reality that one man cannot save another in the Death Zone is proven season after season. Experience has shown that it takes as many as ten skilled climbing Sherpa to get a single disabled climber to a lower elevation—and that is in good weather. It is taxing, tedious, dangerous work. If a climber in the Death Zone cannot walk, he cannot be saved— and there is no point in trying.

Peer never hesitated. He managed to get the nearly dead Tsongba to his feet. How he did that he's never explained, but he pulled the man to the edge of the shelf and single-handedly lowered him down the Hillary Step. He was perhaps the only man on earth capable of the superhuman effort.

Rusty had turned back as well—mere yards from the top of Summit Ridge. His own skilled Sherpa became disoriented in the storm and was never seen again, leaving Rusty to his fate. Somehow Rusty managed to make the correct—and lifesaving—decision.

Coming down the Step, Rusty encountered Peer struggling with the now fully unconscious Tsongba. The men lifted him onto Peer's back and, guided by Rusty, the intrepid Norwegian carried him down to Camp Five where Calvin and three Sherpa were waiting.

In a tent, Cal plunged Tsongba's blackened feet into warm water and applied warm compresses to his dark nose and cheeks. Within days, the valiant Sherpa lost both feet, a hand, and his nose from acute frostbite.

Above, in the freezing storm, Derek and Reggie waited for rescue.

---

Now the most inexcusable event occurred—one for which there have still been no answers. The second Sherpa with Scott, who was still on the Summit Ridge, became separated from the other. The stalwart Sherpa went back for his friend while Scott hurried down the mountain to safety.

Returning from his triumphant conquest of Everest, Scott passed across the shelf and, by his own admission, stumbled upon Derek, whom he said he found alone. He waited with Derek for a time, he told a friend, for oxygen to be brought up to them. The two friends reminisced about their climbing experiences as they waited.

Elsewhere on the mountain, men and women were struggling to escape the storm or floundering within it. Many simply fell into the snow to die. Countless acts of heroism—many no doubt unreported—took place. On the north side, two climbers all but carried a young woman from near the summit down to their camp. Such heroism is expected of the adventurers who climb mountains.

The last man to see Derek alive has never offered an explanation for what happened that day. We know that Derek was conscious and not incapacitated. When it became clear that Tsongba was not going to return, only one course of action remained for a true friend. This man should have done what Peer managed to do. He should have helped his friend down Hillary Step. Once below the Step, it would've taken no time at all to get Derek to the safety of Camp Five and the ministrations of Doc Cal.

But what did this "friend" do? He left—that's what he did. He left his friend on a mountain. He abandoned Derek Sodoc to die.

*〰〰*

To freeze to death is to fall inexorably into the endless sleep. First, the extremities become numb; then you can no longer feel them at all as the body reserves all warmth for the vital core of the body. There is no pain—just an enormous, overarching lethargy. Those dying become very sleepy and must struggle to stay awake. In time, it's simply not worth the effort.

There is no discomfort of any kind. Those who have survived a near-death experience describe such a death as dreamlike. And so Derek Sodoc slipped from this world into the next, slowly embraced by Somnus, the ancient god of sleep—assuming this is the kind of death he endured. What dreams he had we shall never know.

*〰〰*

In the dark, Scott stumbled blindly into Camp Five, announcing to one and all that Derek was dead.

Word of the disaster spread around the world with the speed of light. Millions were stunned by the shockingly abrupt turn of events. One moment, the anchor was describing success and the next he was solemnly announcing disaster and death.

Spontaneous memorial services were held worldwide. A candlelight vigil took place outside SNS headquarters in New York as fans waited for a miracle and assurance that the initial report of Derek's death was in error. But they waited in vain.

We can only imagine the pain endured by Michael Sodoc. We might not like the man, but this was his only son. This should never have happened.

It had been a shock when Tarja set out with her catch to summit Everest because everyone on the expedition knew what she was up to with her fair-haired stud. When she returned, alone and sullen, the only surprise was that she hadn't died on the mountain. But then they say that only the good die young.

Informed of her husband's death, Tarja came out of her tent and cried for the cameras. They were crocodile tears. There been no prenuptial agreement and she stood to inherit an incalculable fortune. You can only ask how sad she really felt. This cunning gold-digger had been trying to land a rich husband for years. She'd finally pulled off the feat and now experienced the warm comfort of her new, vast fortune.

# Derek Dies on Everest

*By Marta Espinoza*
*Sodoc News Service*
*June 13*

"He's dead! He's dead!"

With those words, an unidentified emotional climber broadcast the news soon heard around the world. Adventurer Derek Sodoc was dead—mere yards from the summit of Mt. Everest. According to one source, he succumbed to the elements near the final resting place of legendary climber George Mallory.

Until the tragic news, it was believed that all was well in Derek's final summit push. Even with modern communication, long periods of silence are routine, so it was no great concern when good word failed to materialize from the climbing team.

"He was caught in the worst blizzard in recorded Everest history," said Alpine climber and good friend Peer Borgen who made up part of that team. "We all became separated. There were many deaths."

Over a dozen climbers appear to have perished in the violent storm, making this one of the deadliest ever.

There was no comment from Michael Sodoc, Derek's father and CEO of Sodoc News Service. A close family friend reports he is in seclusion.

# Chapter Eight

# The Ultimate Reality

The drama was not as yet played out. The brave Sherpa, believed to be dead, had spent the night on the summit, searching for his lost friend. Shortly after dawn, he miraculously emerged from the storm and entered the camp. He looked like nothing so much as the Yeti, the ghost monster of the Himalayas. Somehow he'd managed to live through a violent night in the Death Zone.

The blizzard continued that day. Hoping against all odds, Doc Cal and his hearty Sherpa waited for others, but no one came down. Reluctantly, once the storm lifted, they retreated down to Advanced Base Camp where Doc Cal accepted the inevitable. He'd paid his price for dedication, losing toes on his right foot to frostbite.

For some days the expedition, or what remained of it, waited. It had lost its heart in Derek and its soul in Reggie. When it became apparent that no other climbers could possibly reach the summit of Everest that season, all hope of recovering Derek's body was given up. The expedition began its slow, mournful crawl away from the lofty Himalayas.

Tarja spent her days on the sat phone talking to her publicist and God only knows who else. At night, she eased her pain with the services of one of the climbers. Whatever sadness the new widow felt was gone long before she reached Kathmandu.

And so what had begun so auspiciously ended in tragedy. It was a tragedy recorded with the most modern technology. If ever there was a moment in time when we should know exactly what took place, this is it. Instead, we are as much in the dark as we are for so much of history. In this case, we remain uninformed because people refuse to talk.

You can only ask why they remain silent. What are they trying to hide? Why did so many so-called friends abandon Derek in his hour of greatest need? What really happened on the shelf that day? Already rumors drift down from the high regions—stories that suggest something very sinister was afoot that tragic day.

"We know what happened," my Sherpa source told me. "In time, everyone will know and understand. We lost some of our best up there. It is a lesson to every Sherpa. I think you Westerners learned nothing. You still think you own the world."

---

What will happen next? It's hard to imagine that one of the world's richest men would leave his only son up there. With all that money and power, you'd think he'd want his son to have a proper burial. Perhaps he will. We'll see.

And rumors swirl about, as they will, about what really happened, about what Scott and others did and did not do. We'll see about that too.

A fight for the Derek Sodoc fortune began. Michael Sodoc is refusing to give an inch. His wife reportedly despises Tarja. No surprise there. The Norwegian beauty is small fry compared to the senior Sodoc. If she hadn't been his son's wife, he'd swat her like a fly.

But even the all-powerful Michael Sodoc must be careful about public perceptions. Tarja knows that and is banking on it. "She'll get a fortune," a pal says. "She's got one coming legitimately and Sodoc will pay up rather than have her write a tell-all book. She's sitting pretty."

This account may be as close to the truth as we'll ever have—though a chapter or two may yet have to be written. It has been, in its way, a morality tale. If we've learned nothing else, we now know that to be rich and famous and handsome guarantees nothing in life.

All mountains kill, and our greater lesson is that Everest just happens to be the biggest killer of all. On Everest, death is the ultimate reality.

# About the Authors

## Charles G. Irion

Charles G. Irion is an author, adventurer, entrepreneur, and philanthropist. In the 1970s, Irion began his career in commercial real estate development and brokerage. In 1983, he founded U.S. Park Investments, a company that owns and brokers manufactured home and RV communities. In 2007, Irion founded Irion Books and began writing and publishing books. His first book was *Remodeling Hell*—one of four books he authored as part of the Hell Series. This was followed by *Autograph Hell, Car Dealer Hell*, and *Divorce Hell*. Inspired by real-life events, these books are true stories created by actual (hellish) events that infuriated Irion to the point of wanting to expose the demons through his writings. He is donating all of the net proceeds of his Hell Series to victims of fraud.

While writing the Hell Series, Irion began work on the Summit Murder Series. The impetus behind the murder mystery series was his participation in a 1987 expedition to Mount Everest from the China side. Irion couldn't resist creating plot-twisting, adventure-filled stories against the backdrop of the world's deadliest mountains.

Over the past thirty years, Irion has also garnered a large collection of recipes from resident RV campers. More than 350 of these can be found in his book *Roadkill Cooking for Campers: The Best Dang Wild Game Cookbook in the World.*

Irion holds a Masters of Business Administration in International Marketing and Finance from the American Graduate School of International Management and Bachelor of Arts degrees in both Biology and Economics from the University of California, Santa Barbara. As an explorer, Irion has visited more than sixty countries and is an accomplished SCUBA diver. He is also the founder of a children's dictionary charity, a founding member of Phoenix Social Venture Partners, and past president of a local Lions Club. Irion lives in Arizona with his wife, Rose Marie, who he met in Osaka, Japan, at a World Trade Center conference and their beautiful daughter, Chriselle.

To learn more about Charles Irion, please visit: www.CharlesIrion.com

# Ronald J. Watkins

Ronald J. Watkins is an American writer of novels and nonfiction. Watkins has also served as co-author, ghostwriter, collaborator, or editor for more than thirty books. He is the founder and principal writer for Watkins & Associates. In 1993, Watkins published *Birthright*, the saga of the Shoen family, which founded and owned U-Haul International and of the then-unsolved murder of Eva Shoen. When he refused to identify his sources under subpoena, he was twice found in contempt by a federal court, with his position being upheld by the Ninth Circuit on both occasions.

These established case law sustaining the right of authors of nonfiction books to not identify either confidential or non-confidential sources. For Watkins' defense of the First Amendment, he was recognized as a finalist for the PEN/Newman's Own First Amendment Award.

Watkins' first book, *High Crimes and Misdemeanors*, was an account of the impeachment of Arizona governor Evan Mecham.

Written just one year after the events, and based on hundreds of interviews with participants, it remains the definitive account of an American impeachment.

He then authored *Evil Intentions*, the story of the brutal murder of Suzanne Rossetti in Phoenix, Arizona. It was followed a few years later by *Against Her Will*, the story of the murder of Kelly Tinyes in Valley Stream, Long Island, New York. This was the first murder case in the State of New York solved in large part by DNA testing.

In 2003, John Murray (UK) published Watkins' book, *Unknown Seas: How Vasco da Gama Opened the East*. The following year, Watkins was nominated for the Mountbatten Maritime Prize in the United Kingdom. The book has since been published in Portuguese in Brazil and in Czech in the Czech Republic.

Watkins is co-author with Charles G. Irion on the Summit Murder Series, mystery novels set on the highest mountains in the world. In all, the Series is projected to include eight books. He holds a Bachelor of Arts in History and a Master of Science in Justice Studies. Following university, he worked as a probation officer and presentencing investigator for the Superior Court in Phoenix, Arizona. He is a former chief administrative law judge and was assistant director of the Arizona Department of Insurance where he served as Arizona's chief insurance fraud investigator.

Watkins has been called on by the media and has made a number of television and radio appearances, including Dominick Dunne's Power, Privilege, and Justice; PrimeTime! with Tom Brokaw and Katie Couric; Under Scrutiny with Jane Wallace; Geraldo with Geraldo Rivera, and American Forum national radio program.

To learn more about Ronald J. Watkins, please visit:
www.RonaldjWatkins.com

# The Summit Murder Series

Eight plot-twisting mystery novels set against the backdrop of the world's highest and deadliest mountains.

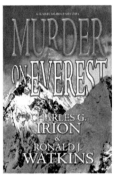
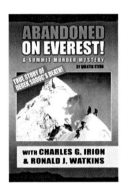

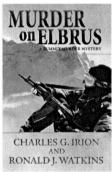

*Murder on Everest*
*Abandoned on Everest, a prequel to Murder on Everest*
*Murder on Elbrus* (Summer 2010)
*Murder on Mt. McKinley* (Winter 2011)
*Murder on Puncak Jaya* (Summer 2011)
*Murder on Aconcagua* (Winter 2012)
*Murder on Vinson Massif* (Summer 2012)
*Murder on Kilimanjaro* (Winter 2013)

www.SummitMurders.com
www.AbandonedOnEverest.com
www.IrionBooks.com